The Man Who Needs You

MIA MAE LYNNE

a "Southern Men Don't Fall in Love" novel

Published by: Book & Spirit, LLC

Cover Credit: Lex Hupertz

Edited by: Lex Hupertz

Copyright © 2010 Chronicles of Fate

ISBN-13: 978-1943651160

ISBN-10: 1943651167

i

DEDICATION

To the almighty God of Love and Light

"Please bless this book so all readers can enjoy in the manner in which the angels and spirit guides have intended."

To my parents Johnnie Mae Parker (May 1, 1937 – April 23, 2013) and Carl Parker (April 5, 1929 – February 25, 2009)

"The lessons you gave me will follow me through eternity."

To my sons Carlos and Marcus

"Follow your dreams and the rewards will be beyond anything you can ever imagine."

To my friend Linda Smithers

"Diamonds are a girl's best friend. Your encouragement and guidance has helped me overcome seemingly impossible obstacles just by being you. You are truly my diamond."

To my friend Melissa Montgomery.

"I admire how you handle any disastrous situation with the grace and poise of the southern belle that you are. You have a gifted ability to capture the lighter side of life and spread sunshine to those who are fortunate to get to know you."

For Noel Marion, my first complete series reader

"Thank you for believing in me and taking the time to inspire me to reach for more."

For my best friend Dolphis Sloan (June 9, 1965 – February 14, 1998)

"As my big brother, you took me under your wing in my teen years and encouraged me to follow your lead in going to the University of Akron. You are a genuinely kind free spirit and even after all these years, you are still dearly missed."

ACKNOWLEDGEMENTS

"For all others who have graciously given their time to support me through the writing process, I humbly express my thanks" – Mia Mae Lynne

Kim, Dawn, Kelli & Marcella

Earth Family

Lex Hupertz

Tiffani Keaton

Nicole Penny

Mandy Varley

Nicole Westbrook

My Tribe

LIGHT WORKERS

"Light workers are those who are brought to earth and are unselfishly dedicated to giving their time to shine their light on humanity and make the world a better place." – Mia Mae Lynne

Debi J. Fellows

Spirals of Spirit, Painesville, Ohio

Effie Kapodistrias

Effie's Divine Celebration, Oakville, ON

Nicole Westbrook

Inner Fyre, Mentor, Ohio

CHAPTER 1

He was making a big mistake.

Marrying that woman instead of her would be his demise.

Nevertheless, she had to be there to see him do it.

He'd been in the running to be husband number three, or so she thought. His wedding announcement came as a big surprise.

She'd captured an invite despite the silent protest of his bride.

Katie Pennington Leigh was a winner and she knew it.

Ms. Lisa may have his attention for now, but it wouldn't last.

This was the first Saturday in February. Who in the hell would get married on a cool grey day?

Doug Bader.

The charming, irresistible bachelor she planned to snag.

Katie snatched through the designer dresses in her closet. Any one of them would make everyone take notice of her instead of his stupid bride. Her

Coco Chanel classic white dress hand-me over from a fashion model friend was the prize of her closet. She fingered the silky-smooth material.

"Ooh," she breathed. "I would look awesome in this."

She pulled the dress out of her closet and held it in front of the mirror.

She remembered the occasion and replaced it.

"Bad luck to upstage the bride in white at her wedding. Anyway, it's a summer dress. I've got enough man trouble without adding a stupid superstition to it."

She spotted a trendy yellow sweater dress. Finally, a good candidate to wear.

"I bought that in Paris last month."

She selected pearl accessories, cream colored two-inch fashion boots with the zipper on the side and a feather tulle bonnet that would draw attention.

"No bonnet." She said in disgust and threw it across the room.

"How dare he marry her!"

She thought Doug understood her commitment to her work. He was the one that wouldn't take her divorce case so *he* could go out with *her*! They'd only went out a couple of times, but still…

Who was this woman and how did she snag him?

She flicked her wrist and looked at the hands of the gold and diamond watch on her arm. "Time to go."

She snatched her purse, marched out of her North Atlanta home, and hopped in the limousine that her daddy loaned her for the weekend. She crossed her legs, leaned back in her seat and pressed the keypad on her phone.

"This is Mel," chirped the friendly voice through the phone.

"It's Katie. On my way to his funeral."

Mel chuckled. "I can't believe you didn't get Doug Bader. If anyone landed him, I thought it would be you."

"Have you seen the papers?" She asked. "The *Atlanta Social Season's* magazine did a follow-up story that was titled: *Atlanta's Most Eligible Bachelor - Caught.* They've even mentioned his wedding on TV in the celebrity news."

"I'm glad you're going. If he comes to his senses and leaves her at the altar, you'll be there to console him."

"Thanks Mel, I have to go. I'll call you with all the details later."

The limousine arrived at Dupree Country Club along with several other expected guests for the wedding. Photographers from the local newspapers snapped photos of the event.

Katie seethed with anger that she wasn't the center of attention. *She'd* expected to be the blushing bride walking down the aisle at *her* wedding with Doug.

She hid her disappointment behind the most beautiful plastic smile that she could span across her face. She mingled with familiar and unfamiliar guests and realized how little she really knew about Doug's social circle.

Working her way through the crowd, she found Harold and his wife. She exchanged pleasantries with them before she excused herself to talk to other guests.

Why waste her time talking to those two?

His wife was pregnant and he wasn't available.

She spotted her coworker, Greg Speaks, across the room and walked over to greet him.

He was single.

African-American.

Executive.

Maybe?

Not a chance. She had standards and one of them was not dating someone that she worked with.

Going through another divorce clouded her judgement and her mind wandered away.

"Good to see you." Greg shook her hand and tapped his cheek against hers.

"You look handsome as ever." She leaned in, lightly, took his hand and caught a whiff of his Versace cologne.

He laughed and stepped back. "Thanks. I hate to cut this short but the groom is pacing the floor, nervous as hell and needs me. We'll talk after the ceremony."

With that said, she watched him maneuver his way through the crowd, extending his hand and shaking it with the guests as he made his way to the groom's dressing room.

She sat down with the rest of Doug's family on the groom's side of the aisle, and waited for the ceremony to start.

***

"Are you coming, Dad? We're going to be late." April shouted.

"I'll be down in a minute," Jack yelled back.

He took one final look in the mirror to see how he looked in his navy-blue suit.

If Paige were here, she'd make him wear cufflinks.

When she was alive, she'd preened over him when he dressed up, made sure his clothes were freshly pressed and his shoes polished. Looking down at the shine on his black leather boots, he smiled. He lifted his head, grabbed his wallet off the dresser, and took one last look around the room. It was time to go before April came to get him.

He whistled a favorite tune as he walked down the stairs hoping that it would lighten his mood. He should be happy that his daughter invited him as her escort to a wedding, so why was he dreading it?

"Do you want me to drive?" April asked.

"You don't have your learners yet."

April chuckled. "I turn fifteen really soon. When are you signing me up for driver's ed.?"

"After you turn fifteen. I'll handle the driving for now."

The ride began silently other than April giving him directions.

"I want you to talk to the guests and not sit in the corner. There's no TV, and watch your alcohol."

"You're beginning to sound like my mother. Have you been talking to her?"

April laughed. "Yes, Grandma is worried about you. She wants you to get out and do healthy activities and so do I."

"I'm going to this wedding, aren't I?"

"But I had to make you go, otherwise you'd be sitting in front of the game."

Jack sighed. He was in a no-win situation with his daughter. He should be grateful for her concern but she was demanding, much like her grandmother. "I'll talk to the guests, April. Happy?"

She took two of her fingers and pointed to her eyes then to his. "I'll be watching you."

CHAPTER 2

Katie sat there, stoic.

Was anyone going to stop this farce?

The wedding was happening before her eyes. She couldn't move. She couldn't scream. All she could do was watch, and then Doug was married.

She got up from her chair to go to the reception still stunned by the fact that he actually married that woman. She mingled with the guests and avoided the newlywed couple. She spotted a familiar face. The woman had light colored hair and a pink corsage on her lapel.

Katie greeted her with a kiss on the cheek. "My, you look lovely today, Ms. Mona. I'm sure you're really happy for your nephew."

"Thank you. You look lovely as well, Miss. Katie." Mona's cheeks were flushed, her eyes glazed over and rolled upwards.

"Ms. Mona? Are you alright? Do I need to call a doctor?" Katie offered her hand in assistance.

Mona accepted her hand and looked directly in her eyes, "You may not get the man you want, but you will get the man who needs you."

Katie's jaw dropped. The loud clamor of the guests faded in the background and her eyes widened as she stared at Mona.

What on earth did that mean?

Had the older woman lost her mind?

I know a good psychiatrist if she needs one.

"Miss Mona, I've been divorced twice. Are you saying that I'll get another shot at this?"

"My dear, what you desire is not what you need. You are destined for another path. Many will be depending on your wisdom and strength. Your value cannot be measured by gold."

Katie was speechless.

Mona shook her head. She perked herself up, straightened the bottom of her skirt and squared her shoulders, "I must go and attend to other guests. You take good care of yourself and remember my words."

She disappeared before Katie could respond.

What did she mean by the man who needs me?

Why can't I get the man I want?

What path is she talking about?

There were too many questions on her mind and Mona didn't offer any answers. She was so shaken by Mona's statements that she hastened to find a ladies' room to freshen up her makeup. She couldn't imagine or digest all that Mona told her.

***

April watched Katie during the ceremony.

She wanted a chance to speak to her.

The woman was beautiful, well dressed, and had a nice smile.

It just seemed natural to follow her to the bathroom.

April wasn't stalking, not really, but she watched the woman applying makeup to her perfectly lined lips in the mirror.

She stared in awe.

***

Katie looked in the mirror and gazed at her appearance before she managed to smile at the young girl behind her. "Are you one of Lisa's soccer players?"

All the teenagers were Lisa's guests according to the gossip she'd overheard. They all called Lisa: "coach," and all of them were grouped together around the outskirts of the reception talking about soccer, boys, and Doug.

The girl looked a little startled that she'd been caught watching Katie, but responded gamely after a moment. "Yes, ma'am, I'm April. I'm sorry for staring, but you are beautiful."

Katie grinned. "And so are you. I'm Katie. You look lovely in that pink dress."

"Are you single?"

Katie paused, turned her head and looked April in her eyes.

The teenager had a sincere expression and anxiously awaited a response.

"Yes, I am." She said, puzzled as to why this teenager would ask that question.

April let out a sigh of relief, smiled, and said, "I would really like to introduce you to my dad."

This is sweet.

A teenager trying to fix up her dad.

I have girlfriends that wouldn't dare fix me up.

Katie smiled, remembering her own father's trouble with women and wishing she'd had the audacity and spunk of the girl before her. She responded, "I would love to meet your dad."

"He's here. Can you come now to meet him?"

Katie's eyes widened but she forced the smile to remain on her face.

"Sure," she looked in the mirror, rummaged through her purse and looked for something, anything to calm her nerves. She didn't know why, but meeting April's dad made her a little nervous and fluttery inside.

Why not? I'm single. Who knows how this will turn out?

"Lead the way."

***

Jack sat through the ceremony and remembered the vows he took with Paige. She had been fond of Lisa. She would have enjoyed seeing her get married.

After the ceremony, April nudged him to get up and mingle with the guests. He congratulated the happy couple and ate a few of the hors d'oeuvres.

"Hi, are you one of the soccer parents?"

Startled by the woman's appearance, he extended his hand, "Yes, I'm Jack. April's dad."

"Ah yes, Lisa talks about her all the time. I'm Terri, Lisa's sister. Are you enjoying the wedding?"

"Yes, very nice and it's nice to meet you."

They talked a few minutes before Terri excused herself to attend to Lisa who was waving her over, and Jack smiled, relieved to have a few minutes to himself in the aftermath.

He found a quiet place to sit and enjoy the music. He looked around to see if April was watching.

Yep.

Caught.

April was headed his way with a woman.

She was an attractive blonde in a yellow dress. He'd noticed her earlier but hadn't taken specific interest.

Now he wished he had.

The closer she came the better she looked.

He rose to shake her hand.

"Dad, this is Miss Katie. Miss Katie, this is my dad, Jack."

He cleared his throat and spoke in a low southern drawl. "It's nice to meet you, Miss Katie."

He was thankful that his daughter talked him into coming to the wedding. If this was what single wedding guests looked like, then he ought to attend weddings more often. He was certainly glad he'd "cleaned up" so he looked his very best.

"It's nice to meet you as well, Jack."

***

Katie assessed his appearance. He had thick black hair, a bushy moustache, square chin, muscular build, and dark brown eyes. The inexpensive watch on his arm was a dead giveaway that he was a working-class man.

Nothing that daddy would approve of.

Always better to be polite though.

***

The introduction didn't seem to be going well. Jack avoided staring at Katie by looking at his daughter. Katie rested back on her heels and looked around the room as if she were trying to assess where the exit signs were.

Katie attempted to put the strap of her clutch purse on her shoulders but realized it was too short so she gripped it tight with both hands in front of her.

Jack cleared his throat and looked at Katie. His deep southern drawl eased over his lips before he could think his question through. "Would you like to dance?"

She loosened the grip on her clutch, glanced over at the pleading look from his teenage daughter, and returned her eyes to his.

"Just this one."

CHAPTER 3

He extended his hand.

She placed hers in his.

Trust.

The song was a slow melodic tune. He turned her around to face him. He placed his hand lightly on her waist. She lifted her hand and placed it on his shoulder. His right hand, her left hand clasped. They swayed together allowing the tune to measure their steps.

He rested his face against hers. He inhaled the sweet smell of her perfume. Strands of her long blond hair bristled against his clean-shaven cheek. He slowed his pace so she could move effortlessly with him.

***

Katie took slow steps under his guidance and relaxed in his arms. It had been a while since she was held this close in a respectable way.

It was almost as if they'd done this dance before. The closer she danced with him, the more she felt each heartbeat against the middle of her breast.

Three songs later, the music stopped. She glanced around and realized she was still at Doug's wedding.

Both stood staring at each other for a moment.

Words formed on her lips but only the air she breathed moved through them.

Thankfully, he found something to say.

"Thank you, Miss. Katie for the dance. I meant no disrespect if I held you too close."

Still staring at him, she stammered, "Well uh, yes uh, I mean, you're welcome."

April appeared next to her dad.

Suddenly, the room felt uncomfortably warm. Katie's face flushed and beads of perspiration formed across her forehead. "I – I think I'm going to need something to drink."

April interrupted. "I'll get it. You stay here and talk to my dad. Dad, do you want a drink too?"

"Uh, yes. Please."

April left the pair standing. Katie wanted to run but her feet were firmly planted on the marble tiled floor.

His smile deepened and his dark eyes steadily gazed into hers. She attempted to look past him and not return the stare. No such luck. His dark eyes mesmerized her.

Damn. He's handsome.

"Doug and Lisa look happy." She blurted out.

Now where did that come from?

"They do."

Katie's throat was dry. Probably from gawking at him for the last five minutes. She felt like a teenager meeting her first crush.

April returned with ginger ale for the both of them.

"Thank you." Katie swallowed the fizzy drink rapidly. The sound that came out of her mouth was somewhere between a frog croak and a pop. She covered her mouth in embarrassment.

April giggled. "Good one."

"Oh, excuse me, I'm so sorry." She blushed, "I was really thirsty."

"It's alright. I like a good belch." Jack said in-between chuckles.

"Well," Katie stammered, "it was nice meeting both of you." She took a step back and looked across the room to see where she could make her departure.

"Don't go yet. Do you like soccer?" April asked Katie.

Now focused on the question from the teenager, she answered. "I'm not sure I've seen the game played before,"

April's eyes lit up. "Oh really. Would you like to come to my soccer game next Saturday? It's a big game. I would love for you to come watch me play."

"April, that's not—"

"But Dad, she's never seen a game before and it's a big game! It would be the best one for her to go to!"

Jack turned from his daughter to stare into Katie's eyes. This glamorous lady would probably turn down the invitation. Seeing the hesitant look on her face, he intervened in order to support his daughter. "The game is really important to April. It would mean a lot if you would come."

***

Feeling the pressure from April and her dad, Katie thought over the invitation.

April appeared to be a very polite and friendly young lady who wanted to teach her to become a soccer fan.

Jack appeared to be very involved in his daughters' activities.

How could she say no to them?

"Sure, I'll come."

She reached in her purse, pulled out a pen and her business card. She wrote her cell phone number on the back before handing the card to April.

"What's an Export Compliance Officer?" April asked.

"I handle our company's policies when it comes to international trade with other companies."

Jack was impressed, "That sounds very important. Are you a lawyer?"

Katie never heard anyone outside of work view her career as important. She felt comfortable telling them more. "No, however, I occasionally confer with attorneys. I also liaise with our shipping department to make sure all of their documentation is correct."

April exclaimed, "Wow, you must be pretty smart."

Katie laughed. "It takes years to learn all of this, and by the time you learn it, it changes."

April nodded before her gaze was drawn away by someone shouting her name from across the hall. "Megan is calling me," she said. "Miss Katie, it was nice to meet you and I hope to see you on Saturday." She pranced off with the crowd of teenage girls and left Katie alone with Jack.

"Do you mind if we sit and chat a moment?" he asked. He picked up her hand ever-so-delicately, and her fingers folded into his effortlessly.

She was mesmerized by his deep southern twang that echoed through her core. "Of course."

She followed him to a quiet place in a hallway with a bench long enough for the both of them to sit.

He looked her in the eyes and said, "You don't have to attend the game next Saturday if you don't want to."

Her calendar was in her car and her entire life was in it. She didn't know if she could go either way, and her schedule was far too important to be interrupted by a teenager's desires. "I promised that I would, but I do need to check my calendar to make sure I'm actually in town. My position requires some travel."

Jack nodded at her response. His gaze didn't leave her eyes and she didn't look away either.

"April is my oldest daughter. She's fourteen. My youngest daughter, May, is six. Their mother recently passed away. They're a little anxious for me to find someone. I think they just don't want me to be alone."

She took note of his sincere tone.

He was a man trying to raise two daughters alone. He must have loved his wife very much.

"I lost my mother when I was twelve. My father never remarried. He's had several girlfriends but none were serious. I believe he didn't want to let go of her memory."

He reached into his back pocket and pulled out his wallet. He handed her his business card. "If you can come to the game, please let me know. I'm sure April would appreciate it."

She smiled and accepted his card.

Landscaping company. Made sense why his hands were rough.

At least he's an owner.

"Of course. I'll let you know" She stood and he stood with her. Katie looked into his eyes and smiled.

He returned her gaze. "Sure thing, Miss. Katie. Have a good evening."

CHAPTER 4

After Katie walked away, Jack returned to mingle with the other guests. Several of them gathered around the groom who had just removed the garter from the bride's leg. He heard April calling for him, waving for him to join the group.

When he didn't move, she came to get him.

"Go, Dad, do it! Catch the garter!"

He let himself be prodded into the line of single men and the DJ announced the count.

"One, two, three."

The black and white laced garter sailed through the air. Jack stepped aside and the man next to him grabbed it. He glanced across the room and caught April's eye. She frowned and marched her way over to him.

"You could have caught that." She crossed her arms and let out a huff.

Before he could respond, April marched off to be with her friends.

He shook his head.

"She's right. You're next."

Startled, he turned to face the woman who spoke. He couldn't imagine why this strange woman would say that or how she was so sure of her statement.

"I'm Mona. Doug's aunt." She extended her hand.

He accepted it and responded, "I'm Jack, father of that precocious teenage soccer player."

She laughed. "Nice to meet you."

He cleared his throat and forced a small smile to his lips. He had no clue what to say. His daughter was a handful and she didn't need any encouragement.

"I'm also known as the crazy aunt in the family. Everyone has at least one."

He laughed and relaxed his shoulders. "No offense, ma'am, but I'm recently widowed. I don't think it's time for me to get married again. Not now. My daughters are my life."

He noticed that they were still holding hands. She reminded him of his favorite Auntie Chessie who was fifteen years older than he was. They always went places together when they were younger. He was *her* baby brother.

Mona pulled her hand away. "One baby girl."

"No, ma'am, I have two girls."

"One baby girl on her way."

He paused and thought about his last girlfriend Barbara. They broke up a few months ago. He'd always worn a raincoat and April would kill him if Barbara was pregnant.

"Not that I know of, ma'am."

"She's coming with your new wife."

"What!" Jack stepped back from the crazy woman.

She couldn't be serious. Barbara and April would kill each other and he wasn't interested in marrying her.

"That's nonsense."

Mona smiled and sang her words in a cheerful melodic tune. "I've got guests to attend to. Enjoy your evening." She stepped away and brushed his shoulder as she walked by.

He was speechless. He couldn't imagine getting married so soon after losing Paige.

"That woman is nuts."

***

"Did you enjoy the wedding?" April asked during the ride home.

"Yes, it was fine." He muttered lowly and focused on the traffic pattern ahead of him.

"Katie was nice."

"Yes, she was."

April reached for the tuner on the radio and changed the station. "Do you think she'll come to my game?"

"I don't know, honey. She seems like a busy woman to me."

"Why don't you call her? I have her card."

"We just left the wedding. Let it rest." Jack turned the station back to his favorite station. He wasn't in the mood to entertain another one of her demands. She was more impatient than usual and interfered with personal space. He caught her looking through his cell phone and examining his pockets.

"You're impossible," she huffed. She opened the glove compartment, closed it, and nestled back in her seat.

"What are you looking for?" he asked. He kept his Trojans in the glove compartment. They disappeared and he suspected she had something to do with it.

"Nothing."

"I'm missing some things that were in the glove compartment. What did you do with them?"

"You broke up with Barbara, and you don't need them. Don't worry; I'm not using them either."

"You stay out of my things and stay away from those boys."

"Why? I learned about sex and babies in school. I'm not letting any of those boys near me to do that. It's disgusting."

He nodded at her response.

She thinks sex is disgusting.

I hope it stays that way for a long time.

CHAPTER 5

She kicked off her boots when she walked into her home and threw her coat on the kitchen chair. The wedding had been exhausting and she didn't understand why.

She plopped on her couch, rubbed her feet and curled them underneath her. She clicked through the channels and decided that nothing interesting was on TV. She drifted off to sleep on the couch.

The phone interrupted her long-awaited rest.

She wiped her eyes and forced herself awake.

"So how was it? Did he marry her?" Mel asked in a half whisper.

Katie sighed, "Yes, he did."

"Details, details please. I expected you to call earlier."

Katie heard snoring in the background. "Who's with you?"

"Oh," she giggled, "Just a friend."

The snoring stopped and a man's voice spoke in the background. She couldn't make out the words but the timbre sounded familiar.

Mel shushed her lover. "Sorry, Katie. Let's do lunch tomorrow at Sandi's. Noon. We'll talk then! Gotta go. Bye-bye."

Mel disconnected before Katie could respond.

That bitch!

She hadn't mentioned that she was dating or having nighttime visitors. Very sneaky, to say the least.

Katie wasn't worried about Mel since Katie didn't have any more husbands or boyfriends for her friends to steal.

She yawned and forced herself from the couch and upstairs. Might as well sleep where she was comfortable at least.

***

Sandi's Place was crowded for a Sunday afternoon. Katie stood in the doorway and stared at her friend, not sure if she wanted to actually talk to the woman anymore.

She'd spent the entire night thinking about that other voice on the line.

The conclusion she'd come to made her stomach ache.

She walked over to her friend's table.

"I'm glad you're here. Kiss. Kiss." Mel took off her shades and extended her arms for a hug.

Katie waved her away.

"What's wrong?" Mel asked and retook her seat.

Katie sat down and looked at Mel. "Was that my dad's voice I heard last night?"

"Err," Mel stammered and put her dark shades on. "I think the salmon looks good."

"You're changing the subject!" Katie exclaimed. "Answer the question."

"Well," she hedged, picked up her martini and took a sip.

"How long?" Katie demanded. "How long have you been sleeping with him? He's my father, Mel!"

Mel sat back in her chair and sighed. "It started about four months ago."

"Are you serious?" Katie banged her fist on the table. "Dammit! I thought I we were friends. You know about my problems trusting people and you're sleeping with my dad and never mentioned it. How disgusting!"

She'd confided her secrets with Mel. How many of those secrets did Mel share with her father? How much did her dad know about her life? Was

Mel happy to tell him the sordid details between the sheets?

Mel placed her hand over her eyes and slouched back in her chair.

"I can't believe you." Katie looked around the restaurant and saw others watching her table and her outburst. She lowered her voice, but the damage was done. "Is there any-fucking-body on the planet that I can trust?"

"Katie wait, let me explain."

Katie shoved her chair backwards from the table and snatched her Louis Vuitton handbag. She rose from her chair with a scowl on her face.

"We're done!"

She marched out of the restaurant and sat in her car. Angry tears streamed down her face. She searched her purse for her planner and was startled by a knock on her window.

"Just leave me the hell alone. I don't want to talk to you now."

Tossing the planner aside, she grabbed her keys from the passenger seat. It took three tries to stick them in the ignition. As soon as the engine started, Mel backed away and ran to her car.

"Fucking bitch!" Katie shouted as she banged her fist on the steering wheel chipping a nail that flicked against the window. "There's no one I can trust."

She skidded off in her car.

***

"You've resorted to fucking my friends now!" Katie shouted through the phone. "Isn't there anything sacred?"

"Watch your tone with me, Katie Louise Pennington. Calm down and explain to me what you are talking about?"

"Do you even know who I'm talking about?"

"Obviously not, Katie!"

Katie was furious with her father. She paced the floor and plopped down on her couch. She stood back up, went to the kitchen and pulled out a shaker for a martini. It was early evening and she wanted something to calm her nerves. "MEL!"

"Ahh," Don replied softly.

Silence.

She continued to make her martini. She added her vodka, ice, and apple martini mix. The ice clacked noisily and she shook every ounce of anger into mixing her drink. She poured the mix into a blush colored martini glass. "Aren't you going to say something? I expected better from you."

"I'll talk to you when you're less angry. Goodnight, Tiger." He disconnected the phone and she couldn't believe it.

"Are you kidding me?" She took big gulps of her drink. The icy cold martini sent cool sensations as it traveled down her throat. She shivered as the iciness flowed through her veins.

She pulled out her planner, skimmed through it and crossed out all plans with Melinda. She rifled back through it and saw blank pages of free time.

"Fill it. I have to fill this time. My life is not an empty calendar. I'm important."

"Dammit! I'm important."

"I have things to do!"

She looked across the coffee table and snatched the purse that she'd taken to the wedding. She fumbled through it for her lip-gloss and noticed Jack's card sticking out of the depths.

"I think I'll give him a call."

CHAPTER 6

Jack rested on the couch in front of the TV late Sunday evening. He could hear the blaring of rock music playing from April's room. May sat next to her dad and read a book for school.

The phone rang.

He reached his hand over to the end table to answer. "Williams' residence, who's calling please?"

"Hi, this is Katie Pennington."

Startled by the sound of her voice, he sat upright on the couch.

May's head tilted upward. She tugged his shirt and whispered, "Who's that?"

His glanced down at May. He pressed his finger to his pursed lips to silence her. "Hello, ma'am. How can I help you?"

"I was calling to get the time and details of the game on Saturday. I have my planner and can check my availability."

"Let me get April for you, hang on one minute," he waved at May who was listening intently to go get her sister.

Katie could hear his daughter yell through the house: "Sissy! Phone for you."

"April will know all the details."

"Oh, thank you."

He heard the pause in her voice, the awkward silence as they waited. "Did you enjoy the wedding?"

"I did. Thank you for the dance."

"My pleasure, ma'am."

Two sets of footsteps bounded down the stairs.

April exclaimed: "Is that her?"

Jack nodded. "Here she is now, Miss Katie." He handed the phone off before he heard the woman's response.

A smile beamed across April's face. "Yes ma'am, this is April. Can you come to my game? I really hope you can be there."

Katie answered, "Yes, I'll be there. Will you please give me the time and directions?"

"It's at 1:00 p.m. at the field in Roswell. My team is in white…"

Before April finished her conversation, he motioned for the phone. April handed it to him.

Jack held the phone while April and May stared at him to see what he would say. He motioned for them to leave the room. They scurried upstairs and the footsteps stopped. He didn't hear them close their room doors so he suspected that they were eavesdropping on the conversation and he carefully continued to talk.

"Thank you for letting us know. April's happy that you'll be there."

"I must go. I still have a few things to accomplish before I go to work in the morning."

"Goodnight, Miss Katie."

***

Katie arrived at the soccer game fifteen minutes before it started. She'd never attended a soccer game before and realized too late that she was overdressed.

She wore a modest knee length pink sweater dress with white polka dots and the length of her trench coat was down to her ankles.

She asked another spectator for directions to April's field. She carefully walked over but her two-inch heels sank in the grass with every step.

Several parents turned around to look at her as she walked over to the field.

She straightened her shoulders and pretended not to notice.

As Katie approached April's field, she caught a glimpse of a hand waving. Her eyes followed the gesture. She recognized April, smiled and waved back, steadying her balance while walking closer.

A dark-haired man closed the distance and stood in front of her.

Jack was wearing a jacket with a dark green polo shirt underneath, jeans and tennis shoes. He smiled and extended his hand. "I'm glad you could make it. I brought a chair for you to sit in."

"Thank you. I would've dressed more appropriately had I known the attire. I've never been to a soccer game."

She followed Jack to the sidelines of the field. He picked up the dark green folding chair that rested on the ground. He offered his arm and she used it to balance herself to settle in the chair. She looked around and didn't notice another chair.

"Aren't you going to sit down?" She asked.

"I can never sit through these games." He responded.

She looked across the field and saw Doug Bader approaching her.

He nodded at her and extended his hand to Jack. "Game on?"

Jack smiled and shook his hand back. "April's ready. This will be a tough one though."

Doug's eyes returned to Katie.

She attempted to stand up.

"Stay seated. The game's about to start." Jack advised.

"It's good to see you again. I have to find a seat. Excuse me." Doug left the couple, climbed the bleachers and sat with a few other parents. Katie turned her gaze back to the field to watch the play.

Jack spent most of his time with Katie explaining the rules of the game. She was very engrossed with the action at hand. There were twenty-two girls running around chasing a ball on a field.

"The game stopped. Is it over?" She asked.

Jack squatted down next to her side to more easily speak with her. "No, ma'am, it's half time."

The girls from both teams returned to their respective benches.

A little girl with long dark hair and a pink jacket skipped towards them.

She hugged Jack.

"Where have you been? Did you watch your sister play?" He asked.

"I was at the playground."

"This is Miss Katie. Katie this is my youngest daughter, May."

May looked at Katie, smiled and climbed into her lap.

Katie was a little surprised that she would be sharing a chair with his daughter. Jack shooed her away.

"May, please leave her alone."

"It's fine." Katie dismissed his concern and spoke to May. "How are you?"

She faced Katie and asked, "I'm fine. Are you here with my daddy?"

Katie smiled back at her. "Your sister invited me to watch her play. Do you play soccer as well?"

"Yes, ma'am, but my season is over. Are you coming to eat with us later?"

"I don't know. Would you like for me to come?"

"Yes, ma'am, and sissy would too." May turned around and leaned her back against Katie's chest.

His eyebrows narrowed with concern, "Miss Katie may have plans later. Please don't bother her with that."

"It's okay," Katie replied. "I can come if the girls want me to join them for lunch."

His cheeks softened and his shoulders relaxed. "I'm sure they'd love that."

***

The referee blew his whistle and the girls shook hands on the field.

The game was over and April's team was cheered through their two-goal victory.

Katie waited with Jack and May for April to join them.

"Miss Katie, did you see my goal?" April lightly hugged her dad and Katie. "I'm drenched. I don't want you to get wet."

"I certainly did." She waved away a pesky fly that flew across her face. "Please, both of you just call me Katie. Your father explained the game to me. Your team must be very proud of you."

"Thank you. I'm so glad you came." April tugged on her pink Livestrong wristband. "Can we go eat now? I'm starving."

"Lou's Steakhouse?" Jack suggested and picked up April's soccer bag.

"You bet," April answered. A few of her teammates walked by and she waved at them.

"I've never heard of Lou's Steakhouse." Katie remarked.

"It's one of my favorite places to eat." May held her dad's hand and smiled.

"Why is that?" Katie asked.

"It has everything you could imagine."

Katie smiled. "Then Lou's it is."

"Follow me." Jack led the group to the parking lot.

***

Katie drove her car separately.

She followed the girls and their dad to the restaurant. After she arrived, she soon regretted accepting the invitation because the place was crowded. Several customers stood in line and waited to get inside the building.

The foursome joined the line and May talked away at them as they waited.

"I'm going to own a restaurant like this one," she said. "I want my customers to eat lots of different food."

"I get to help," April chimed in. "I'll do your books. I think I want to be a CPA like my coach. I like math." April reached behind her head and tightened the band on her ponytail.

Jack turned to Katie "I love my daughters." She opened her mouth to respond but all she saw was the dark brown pupils in his eyes.

Wow.

He loves his daughters.

This is their favorite place to eat and he asked them where they wanted to go.

"Yes, I can see that you're devoted to them."

They finally entered the building. The line inside the restaurant was as long as the line outside.

The place was noisy.

Two cashiers were at the end of the line. Kids scampered through the restaurant. Servers refilled drinks and busboys cleared plates. Kitchen helpers refilled empty food on the buffet. One chef was at a station and carved three different meats.

Most of the tables were taken. Big groups of people were in the private section. Every walk of life plowed through each of the dishes on the buffet.

What do I do?

I'm not used to this.

April handed Katie a serving tray. She hadn't seen one of those things since she left college. She never imagined that she would be dining in a cafeteria again.

They walked through the line and gathered plates, cups, and silverware. Jack paid for lunch and the four-some located an empty table. The waitress brought rolls. April rose from the table and walked toward the buffet.

May nudged Katie.

"Have you been here before?" May asked.

"No, I haven't." Katie answered.

"I'll show you around." May stood with her plate in hand and motioned for Katie to follow.

Katie watched in horror as people scurried around the buffet and dumped heaps of food on their dishes. May was accurate in her information. This place had all kinds of food. May loaded her plate with chicken, corn, and macaroni & cheese.

"Aren't you going to eat a green vegetable? That would be better for you. Let's get a salad."

"Okay," May replied mournfully, "I guess I have room on my plate for it."

They walked over to the salad bar. Katie selected leafy green vegetables and a light dressing. She had a sensitive stomach and hoped she wouldn't get sick with all of this activity around food. They returned to the table.

Katie encouraged May to taste the greenery and she happily obliged. April talked about the game. Jack spoke very little and allowed the girls to lead the conversation.

She felt like she was a part of this family.

That's ridiculous.

I just met everyone.

I'm a woman with a full-time career. I don't have time for a family.

As Katie drifted back to the present, she caught a glimpse of him staring at her again. Each time she caught him; he'd smile back or look at the girls.

May picked up a piece of lettuce and dipped it in the Italian dressing. "Mrs. Simmons said that if I want to be a chef that I have to try lots of new things even if I don't like them."

"That's good." Jack said and continued to chew on his morsel of chicken breast.

"Your makeup is so pretty. Can you teach me how to do that?" April asked in-between chews on her slice of buttered bread. "Please."

Katie looked at Jack while she answered April's question. "I can if it is okay with your father."

He stopped mid-chew, picked up his napkin and covered his mouth. "Maybe."

April dismissed his response. "There's a Valentine's dance at school next Friday. Will you help me shop for it?"

I love shopping!

Niemen Marcus, Gucci, Saks…

Don't commit. The Planner rules!

"I have to check my calendar."

Jack frowned. "Do you always live by your calendar or is that your standard answer?"

Katie narrowed her eyes and pursed her lips. She met his stare with her cold sea green one. "Yes, I do check my calendar often. I attend many events. If I don't check my calendar then someone is upset that I made a promise that I couldn't keep. I try to stay true to my word."

Jack nodded, his face smoothing as though he understood her answer, respected it.

"Can I shop too? I want new clothes." May asked.

Katie smiled and answered her young dinner companion. "If it is okay with your dad, I'll take you both tomorrow for lunch and shopping. I'll clear my calendar if there is a conflict."

She looked at Jack. He smiled and savored his last forkful of mashed potatoes.

Katie's plate was still half-full of the green salad that she'd selected from the bar. She wiped the Lite-French dressing from her mouth and placed the napkin on the table. She looked at her watch and rose from her chair. "I have to go. It is getting late and I do have another appointment. I will see you ladies tomorrow."

"Don't go yet. We didn't have dessert," April said.

"I can't have dessert. I'll never fit into this dress if I do."

"Then have some fruit." May said. "Fruit is good for you and you didn't eat much food."

"The girls are right." Jack added. "That wasn't a well-balanced diet. I don't think you ate any protein."

Jack stood up and Katie sat down. He returned to his seat.

What the hell just happened?

She'd walked out of six-person negotiations when they didn't adhere to her schedule but she stayed because they begged her to?

"I'll get dessert." May offered.

"I'll go with you." April stood up and went with her sister.

"I know you have another appointment." Jack said dryly. "So, make your escape now before the girls come back."

"I can't do that. I'll have a few pieces of fruit and I'll call my next appointment and let them know I'll be late." She picked up her purse, pulled out her phone and stood up. "I'll be right back."

Jack stood up as well. "Thank you."

She smiled at him. "You're welcome."

CHAPTER 7

Jack normally spent his Sundays working in the yard. Since he knew that Katie was coming over, he made it a point to be in the house when she arrived.

The doorbell rang and Katie was on time, as she promised.

"I'm coming," he shouted.

He opened the door and was stunned by what he saw.

Katie walked in with her hair pulled back in a bun. Underneath her trench coat, she wore a navy blue pantsuit, navy fashion boots, white blouse, and pearl earrings with a matching necklace. She was dressed more for a corporate dinner than shopping.

He was unable to take his eyes off her as she entered the room.

"Are the girls ready to go?"

Before he could answer, his daughters rushed down the stairs, one in front of the other. May was dressed in faded blue jeans with a matching pink sweater and April was dressed to match with a purple sweater.

"Were we supposed to dress up? I can go change." April said.

"No, what you're wearing is just fine. You'll be trying on lots of clothes."

Jack asked, "How much money do they need?"

"They don't need any. This shopping excursion is my treat."

He shook his head, "No, ma'am, I'll give them some money."

He slipped a wad of cash into April's hand. He was reluctant to allow them to go, but the girls needed a mother figure. Since Katie was willing to give up her time to devote attention to them, he wanted to take advantage and not interfere.

"You look a little uncomfortable. Do you want to come with us?" Katie asked.

"Shopping?" He raised his eyebrows. He didn't expect to be included.

"That's a great idea!" April exclaimed. "You need new clothes too."

"Yes, Daddy. Come with us."

"We can wait for you if you aren't ready." Katie smiled and played with the pearl earring in her ear.

He hesitated but he couldn't say no to the pleading looks on his daughter's face. "Okay, I'll be ready in ten minutes."

**

Everyone realized that shopping would be more fun if they ate first. Katie recommended lunch at Imbrecia's Italian Restaurant.

The dining room setting was formal. Black napkins and polished silverware were set upon a table covered in white linen. Five-course place settings included bread plates and water glasses.

Other than company dinners, Jack didn't have much exposure to formal dining. He felt completely out of his element sitting in the restaurant in his old jeans and button down. His two preferred places to eat were at the kitchen table and in front of the TV.

Katie placed her napkin in her lap and motioned for the girls to follow her lead. Jack placed his napkin in his lap as well.

Each person picked up his or her menu. Most of the menu items were in Italian with English explanations below the dish.

He rubbed the bristly hair of his chin and studied the menu carefully. He glanced over at Katie and noticed the calm smile on her face.

She turned to him and asked, "Do you know what you want to order?"

He cleared his throat and gripped the menu tight. He felt nervous and didn't understand why. "No, ma'am. What do you recommend?"

April interjected, "I don't know what to order either."

"The spaghetti looks good," May offered. "Do I have to eat a salad?"

The waiter arrived while they were discussing the selections. He described the specials of the day and left the table which allowed them more time to consider their options. Katie explained the table settings to the group.

May exclaimed, "Wow, I didn't know forks had different jobs."

April chimed in as well, "I didn't either. You'll tell us what silverware to use when our lunch gets here, won't you?"

"Yes, I will."

May asked, "Why aren't you married?"

April glared at her sister. "You aren't supposed to ask that."

"It's ok. I have been married before but it didn't work out."

"I'm glad you're not married." May rocked in her seat.

"Me too." Jack muttered and hoped no one heard him.

Katie glanced over and smiled.

Damn. She heard it.

"I can't wait until this dance. All of my friends are going," April said.

Katie folded her hands beneath her chin and looked at April. "I'll make sure you look your best."

"Can you come over Friday and help me dress too?" April asked.

Katie responded with certainty. "I will be at your house on Friday no matter what's on my calendar."

***

"It's your turn, Daddy." April exclaimed. "I've got everything I need."

They were at a bench in the mall in front of a men's store. Jack watched the bags as the girls went with Katie to different stores and purchased clothes. The shopping trip was ending and May looked like she was tired. She sat beside him and rested her head on his arm.

"It's getting late and I'm sure Miss Katie has other plans."

Katie pulled out her planner and skimmed through it. Her evening was free. She was in her world, and shopping was her favorite pastime. "If you want to try something on then I'll stay."

May perked up and hugged her dad. April leaned over and whispered in his ear. "I want my dad to take care of himself."

"Okay." He said.

"Daddy lost weight." May said and stood up from the bench. "He needs new clothes."

"You did?" Katie asked.

Jack nodded. "Yes, ma'am."

"Well," she folded her arms across her chest, "it's definitely time for a new wardrobe then."

The group entered the men's store and searched through the racks for clothes. The selection was narrowed down to a few pairs of shirts and jeans.

He came out of the dressing room and the girls assessed his outfit.

"He looks great, doesn't he?"

Katie stopped pulling through racks and stared with her mouth agape. She delicately placed her hand over her heart and gasped.

Wow, he is really handsome!

He'd donned a red and black plaid shirt with straight leg navy blue jeans. With his straggly moustache and dark hair, he looked like a lumberjack, albeit a sexy one.

"Yes, he does."

CHAPTER 8

"Why do I have such a hangover?" Katie groaned as she woke up Monday morning to get dressed for work.

She hadn't done anything crazy, just soccer and a shopping trip.

She shook her head and got ready for work.

Late that afternoon, Katie compiled a report and highlighted items to be revised. She reviewed her calendar and scheduled meetings.

Her office phone rang. "Export Compliance, Katie speaking. How may I assist you?"

"Hi Katie, it's April."

Katie stood and looked out of the window, oddly pleased to have the younger woman on the phone. "Hi April, how are you?"

"Fine," there was a pause, and Katie heard the hesitation on the line, "but I need a really big favor."

"Anything you want."

She'd grown fond of April and her family.

They'd had such a great time yesterday.

She realized that she'd been stuck in her own selfish world for so long that she missed the pleasure of interacting with close family members.

"Can you take me to soccer practice? Dad is working late and I don't have anyone else to ask for a ride."

"Have your dad call me. I'll come get you if he agrees."

"Okay."

Ten minutes later, her office phone rang again.

"Export Compliance, Katie speaking. How may I assist you?"

"Hi Katie, it's Jack."

She leaned back in her chair and twisted the phone cord around her finger. A smile swept across her face. She crossed her legs and twisted side to side in her chair. That deep southern voice sent a heated rush through her body and summer was four months away.

"Yes, Jack. What can I do for you?"

"I don't mean to intrude on your personal time. April doesn't have anyone to take her to soccer practice. I take her when I can. I told her to miss it but she insists on going."

Katie flipped through the pages of her calendar. There was an art show but she could miss it. April needed her and she intended to make herself available.

"Yes, I'll take her."

"Thank you, Miss Katie."

***

Katie wrapped up early so she could be at April's home on time to take her to practice. She pulled in the driveway fifteen minutes early.

April locked the door to the house, rushed down the driveway, and hopped in the car.

"Where's May?"

"She's next door with Ms. Simmons. I'll give you directions to the field."

"Do we have time to stop by my house first? I want to change out of my work clothes. It's on the way to the field."

"Sure, that's fine." April said and flipped her ponytail around her shoulder. "I'd love to see where you live."

"We'll be there soon. I live ten minutes away from the field."

Katie pulled into the drive and retrieved the mail from her dented black mailbox. The flag was missing and the flap was crushed inward.

"I'll have to get that fixed." She muttered. She passed the mail to April. "Will you hold this please?"

"Sure."

They drove up the driveway and stopped in front of her three-car garage.

"You live here?"

"Yes." Katie answered. She pressed the garage opener and pulled through the center door. Once she parked, she extended her hand to April. "I'll take that. Come in with me. It will only take a moment."

"Okay." April answered and gave the mail to her.

Katie entered the house through the garage door that led to a large foyer. "Make yourself at home. I'll be down in a flash."

She rushed upstairs, threw off her work clothes, and grabbed a pink jogging suit from the closet. She pulled out her dresser drawer and selected a long sleeve sweater to go underneath her jogger.

***

Katie drove April to the field and parked her car.

"You're staying for practice, aren't you?"

"Sure."

April hugged her and ran to the sidelines where her team was warming up.

Katie sat in the car and took a few calls from the office. The flashing red light signaled that she had to finish her conversation fast. "Katrina, I've gotta go. Dead battery. Talk soon."

She looked at her watch and realized she'd missed most of April's practice. She got out of the car, walked towards the field and found a seat on a bleacher close to April's team.

She looked up as Doug approached her.

"I see you're back. Are you a girls' soccer fan now?"

Katie laughed. "April didn't have a ride to practice. She called and I was available."

"Oh, I see." He climbed the bleacher and sat near the top next to a male parent.

He seemed content to leave her alone, so she looked across the field to the girls running laps.

April waved and smiled at her.

She noticed an African American male and a younger African American teenager approaching the bench from a distance. She heard Doug's voice call out to them.

"Hey Greg, Warren, over here."

Greg and Warren approached the bleachers and stopped to see her first.

"Katie Leigh, what brings you to soccer practice?" Greg extended his hand.

"April called me and asked if I could give her a ride." She accepted his handshake. His hand was smooth and his grip was firm and light.

"This is my little brother, Warren. I'm part of the Big Brother's program. Warren, this is Miss Katie."

"Hello, Miss Katie." Warren extended his hand to her. Another firm handshake.

He's taking notes well from Greg.

Her father always said that you could tell a good man by his handshake.

Katie was impressed.

"Are you in high school?" She asked.

"Yes, ma'am, I graduate next year. Greg is teaching me about marketing. I think I want to go to college and study that. His Jaguar is all that."

Katie laughed.

Doug joined the group and asked, "Do you and Warren want to join Lisa and me after practice for dinner?"

Greg motioned to Warren and asked, "Do you want to go?"

"Yea, as long as you're buying."

Greg laughed. "It will take a week's pay to feed your bottomless stomach."

Warren's fist lightly jabbed Greg's arm. "Don't play me like that. You got that kind of money."

Greg doesn't flinch at the punch and glared at the teenager before responding. "Warren and I will go. He has homework that I have to help him with so it will have to be a quick bite."

"I'll let Lisa know after practice. Do you and April want to join us?"

Katie smiled at Doug. "Thanks for the offer, but I can't. April's father is waiting for her. We should do it another time though. It would be fun."

***

The aroma of garlic and thyme wafted through the air of the Williams' household.

"What's for dinner?" April called out. She beckoned Katie to follow her to the kitchen.

They overheard the conversation from the living room as they approached.

"No, you have to add more garlic. It tastes better that way," May said.

"Not too much please," he replied.

"It'll taste great. I promise." May passed him the jar of garlic.

He scooped out a teaspoonful and stirred it in the pot.

April stood in the doorframe with Katie behind her. "I'm home and Katie's with me."

Jack turned his head over his shoulder and smiled. "Can you stay for dinner?"

Katie combed her fingers through her hair, "I don't want to intrude. I really need to prepare for work tomorrow."

April pleaded, "Please stay. I really don't want you to leave yet."

It's sweet that April wants to spend more time with me.

"Please stay," May said sweetly, "I taught daddy how to cook spaghetti."

May really knows how to turn on the charm.

"Yes, ma'am." With a smile and a wink, he folded the light blue dishtowel in his hand. "We'd be honored if you would join our family for Italian night." He waved the cloth with a flourish and bow, eyes meeting hers as he rose, holding her captive to his stare.

And she learned it from her dad.

Katie reached into her cream-colored tote bag, pulled out her planner and leafed through it. She found her events for the evening and placed the planner back in her bag.

Nothing important. Just more work. I'll stay up late and get it done.

"Okay, but I can't stay late."

Jack's smile stretched his thick moustache across his face and he folded his arms across his chest.

Katie sucked in her cheeks and forced herself not to return the smile or acknowledge the blush that reddened her face and neck.

"Everyone has to wash their hands first. Especially you sissy since you've been playing in the mud." May said.

Katie chuckled at the demanding voice coming from a grade-schooler. "Yes, ma'am. I'll wash my hands."

After everyone cleaned up for dinner, Katie sat in her designated place. The kitchen was simply decorated in a mushroom theme and painted in a light green.

An interior decorator could do wonders.

May placed a plate of spaghetti in front of her and Jack poured her a glass of sweet tea. She picked up the fork and spoon. She accepted the paper towel from April. It was used in place of a napkin for the messy spaghetti fare.

"This is too much food." Katie complained.

Jack said gruffly, "Eat what you can. You could use a little weight."

"What!" Katie exclaimed.

Does he know how hard it is to keep this weight down?

This meal could blow several calories in my diet if I'm not careful.

"Daddy!" April shouted, "You aren't supposed to say that."

"I'm sorry, Miss Katie, if I offended you."

She twirled a small serving of spaghetti onto her spoon. As she opened her mouth to savor the first morsel, three pairs of eyes stared at her. She inhaled the aroma of garlic and oregano. In went the first bite. "This is delicious. Do you have any salad?"

Jack answered, "We didn't get salad. Sorry. Next time you come we'll have it."

"You can come to dinner tomorrow, can't you?" May asked. "I can teach you how to cook. Ms. Simmons next door and my grandma taught me." May twirled her fingers through one of her pigtails.

"I know. You have to check your calendar." April grumbled.

"Girls, please don't pressure Katie. I'm sure she has plans. It must be a hell of a life to be run by a calendar."

Katie dabbed her napkin across her lips. "I learned how to use a planner in college. I missed many activities because I either forgot or double booked. Planning has saved me from a lot of embarrassment."

Her phone rang and she apologized, reaching for her purse and excusing herself from the table. "Sorry, it's a call from the office. It will only take a minute. I promise."

She stood up and went into the living room.

Five minutes later, May tugged on her shirt.

"Your food is getting cold." She scowled with her arms folded. "I made this especially for you."

"Eh, Katrina. I have to go. My hostess wants to start her dinner party and she's waiting for me. I'll call you after I leave."

Katie disconnected the phone and followed May back to the food. Jack took Katie's plate and gave her a disapproving look. "I'll warm this up for you."

"Yes, uh, thank you. I apologize for the interruption. I was expecting the call earlier."

"I made dessert too." May said. "I hope you like chocolate."

Jack brought Katie her spaghetti and she took several paper towels to cover her white blouse. One ounce of spaghetti on it and she'd be buying a new one.

"May, I insist that you put some of this away for me if you want me to have dessert. I have a strict diet and have to watch my calories."

April said, "I see, Coach Lisa is always talking about diet. No pop, lots of carbs, on and on."

After eating a portion of spaghetti as big as the palm of her hand and half of the piece of bread that was served to her, May brought the chocolate pudding pie to the table. April served everyone and Katie took her first bite.

She breathed her words through the air with a light, soft moan "This is so good. I'm going to pay for this."

May clapped her hands. "Goodie. It's a new recipe."

CHAPTER 9

After Katie left, Jack cleaned up the dishes and April disappeared to her room to do her homework. May was tired so she went upstairs as well.

Jack went into the living room and relaxed on the couch in front of the TV. He thought about grabbing a beer from the fridge but instead was summoned by May.

"Daddy, come here please,"

He rose from the couch and climbed the stairs. May was sitting up in her bed with a coloring book on her lap. He sat beside her.

"What is it pumpkin?"

"When can I go to cooking school? Mommy said she would look into it and she's not here."

Tears dropped from her eyes. She wiped them away with the back of her hand. He hugged his daughter.

"I promise I'll look into it."

***

Jack went back downstairs to the fridge to grab that beer he had a taste for. Just as he opened the door, April shouted for him. She bounded down the stairs and met him in the living room.

"Daddy, the ODP tryouts are coming up. Do you think you can take me?"

"April, that's a lot of soccer. I can hardly get you to regular practice. How am I going to get you to more?"

"Being in the Olympic Development Program will boost my chances for college soccer. You have to take me. I can make this team." April looked her dad square in the eyes. She wasn't backing down.

"No. That's more money for soccer. May wants to go to chef school. I'm not independently wealthy." He wasn't backing down either. He wasn't sure how he was going to work out the schedule between the girls and he was the only parent available to take care of the both of them.

"I'll be driving soon. I'm turning fifteen in two months. I can drive myself to practice."

"Let's take care of May's need first. You have an outlet, she doesn't."

"I'll drive her to chef school. Just let me do ODP. Tryouts are this summer and I should have my learners permit and license by fifteen and a half."

"Let's discuss it closer to tryouts. I can't handle this right now. Go finish your homework so you can go to school in the morning."

"Daddy, you're impossible." April stormed up the stairs and left him alone in the living room. Back to the kitchen to get that beer. One more interruption and he was going to explode. The ringing phone was the last straw.

"What!" he growled.

"It's Katie. Are you okay?"

Jack let out a huff and settled his frustration.

"I'm fine."

"April left her cleats in my car. When does she need them? I can bring them by after work tomorrow. Is that okay?" He could hear the anxiety and stress in her voice.

"If you come back here, you'll have to plan to stay for dinner. The girls will insist. And I know what you're going to say."

She laughed. "I'm checking it now as we are speaking. I'm cancelling those plans. I'll be there tomorrow for dinner with cleats in hand."

***

Jack arrived home early from work. Mrs. Simmons and May were in the kitchen preparing dinner. May blended the ingredients for meat loaf and Mrs. Simmons chopped potatoes.

"Hi, Daddy."

"Heller, Jack."

"Hi, pumpkin. Mrs. Simmons. I'm going up to change."

He told the girls last night that Katie was coming to dinner. On his way up the stairs, he collided into April.

"I picked out your clothes. I want you to look nice when she comes."

With a half-crooked smile, he said, "You did."

"I did. Now go change," she ordered.

He looked at the faded blue jeans and light blue polo shirt on the bed. April selected his favorite belt, dark socks and even his underwear. She laid out his Armani cologne too.

"I've got to start locking my room. This isn't right. My daughter shouldn't be in my underwear drawer."

He jumped in the shower and allowed the steam to wash away the labor of a hard day's work. This would be four days in a row that she'd spent time with his family.

Gripping the bar of soap, Katie's image came to mind. She had a nice figure except she could use more fat on her behind. Shapely legs too. As he lowered his washcloth, he was slowly beginning to rise...

The knocking at the bathroom door startled Jack so bad that he dropped the washcloth. The bar of soap thumped against the tile and just missed his big toe. He clutched at his heart in panic. "What?!"

"Are you ready yet?" April shouted through the door. "She's coming soon."

"Get out of here," he shouted angrily. "I'll be down in thirty minutes."

"Fifteen and you better look good."

"Arrrrgh" he groaned. He grabbed the washcloth from the bottom of the shower and wiped his eyes. "That kid is just like her grandmother. Three more years and I'm sending her off to college. Far, far away..."

***

"Woo wee. Don't you look nice?" April exclaimed as Jack came down the stairs. "I love you." She kissed his cheek.

The phone rang and he answered.

"I'm running late. Crisis at the office. I'm stuck in traffic and by the way it looks right now, I'm an hour away."

"Take your time."

April jerked his sleeve "What did she say?"

"Hold on a minute, Katie," Jack relayed the news to April. "I'm back."

"I'll call when I get closer."

***

An hour and a half later, Katie drove up to the Williams' household still talking to the office when she got out of the car in front of the house. Katie paced, trying to wrap up the conversation before going inside.

"Katrina, please listen to me. I can't spend any more time on this. Let me involve Arthur." She turned around and bumped into Jack who'd snuck up on her when her back was turned.

He held her stare. "Ready to eat?"

She stared back into his eyes unable to further her conversation. She was enchanted with the intensity of his gaze. Her hand lifted absent thought and placed itself in the middle of his chest. The throbbing of his heartbeat pulsed against her fingers. Katrina was still talking and Katie didn't hear a word.

"Tell her goodbye," he half-whispered. "You'll talk to her later."

She swallowed hard as if that were going to bring her back to reality and burst her growing attraction for the family man.

"Katrina, I've got to go."

Embarrassed, she quickly pulled her hand from his chest and moved her eyes to look anywhere but back into his.

He cleared his throat and stepped back.

He was still far too close; he felt far too close.

"I think we're being watched."

She turned and looked at the house.

April and May had their hands and noses pressed against the window. May darted away first but April was a little slower to leave.

He took a step to the side and extended his arm to escort her inside.

***

Katie stopped to freshen up in the bathroom before eating with the family. While applying her makeup, rampant thoughts raced through her mind about her encounter with Jack moments before.

What was that about?

I rarely let a man cut my call short no matter who he is.

I'm in control dammit.

I'm Katie Louise Pennington. I'm wealthy.

Why am I here?

And why, dear God, why is this ordinary man so attractive?

She shook her head, smacked her raspberry glossed lips, and exited the bathroom.

She took her reserved place at the table and noticed only one place setting.

"Is it just me eating?" she asked.

"Yes." He answered. "April has homework and May needs to be in bed in an hour."

"I'm so sorry. I just have so many things to do. I try to fit in as much as I can."

April was near the microwave when it beeped. She brought Katie a plate of meatloaf and gravy. This time, the portion size was much smaller than they served before. Katie was thankful.

"You remembered." She smiled.

"I wanted you to have room for dessert." May said. "I made apple cobbler."

Oh boy.

She was going to have to start skipping lunch or go to a liquid diet for her first two meals of the day.

"Thank you. I'll make sure that I have room for it."

CHAPTER 10

There was a heavy thunderstorm on Friday afternoon when Katie took off from home to go to the Williams' household. She wanted to be at April's house as early as possible to help her prepare for the Valentine's Day dance.

Sitting in traffic, her phone rang again. They must be taking turns. She hadn't talked to Mel or her dad all week and they both called daily.

"I'm not in the mood for this."

She ignored the phone and turned up the radio. Normally she would be talking to the office, but today she just needed time to herself.

She arrived at April's house dressed in more comfortable attire than what she'd worn before. She wore a V-neck red sweater dress with a loose belt. She carried a black Gucci purse and wore black laced boots. Her makeup was placed to perfection.

Under a soaking wet umbrella, she proceeded to ring the doorbell.

"I'm coming."

Jack answered the door.

Her eyes met his.

One soft flutter raced through her heart. His bushy moustache spanned across his face when he smiled. His dark scraggly eyebrows could use a trim but they showed character, divine masculinity.

Not again.

"Hi, Jack. Where are the girls?" She said, breaking the trance that started between them. She was getting the hell out of this house when she was through with April. She would be safer far away from him.

"May is spending the night with a friend. April's upstairs waiting on you." He welcomed her inside and she followed him upstairs to April's room. The music was loud but she could hear April singing when she approached the door.

When the door opened, April stopped and rushed to hug Katie. "I'm so glad you could make it!"

Katie looked at the overnight bag packed on April's bed. "Are you spending the night somewhere?"

"My friend Britney asked me to sleep over at her house after the dance. Dad said it was okay."

***

While Katie helped April prepare for the dance, Jack half-slept on the couch watching TV.

He was just reaching a light doze when the doorbell rang and he got up to answer.

"Hi, Britney. April should be down in a minute."

April and Katie rushed down the stairs. He was pleased with the attire Katie chose for April's dance. His daughter was dressed as a fourteen-year old girl should be. She was not overly made up and her hair was let down. The black leather skirt was slightly above the knee. Her red sweater matched the thick stockings and her front laced boots with two-inch heels reached mid-calf.

No arguments from him.

April made the introductions, "Britney, this is Katie."

"Oh," Britney said. "Is she—?"

April interrupted, "Yes, I'll tell you later." With a kiss on her dad's cheek, she rushed Britney to stand by the door.

"Both of you have a good time. Tell your parents I said hello, Britney."

"Yes, sir."

The girls left.

Jack and Katie stood in the foyer in silence.

She forced a breezy laugh between her lips. "My job is done. I'll see you another time." She moved to find her umbrella and makeup bag.

"Have you eaten?" He asked.

"No, but I can get something on the way home."

"I actually have a little something in the kitchen if you want to stay."

"Well—"

"I know you have to check..."

She interrupted him before he could finish. "I'll stay."

The corners of his dark brown eyes curled upward, his shoulders relaxed, and he smiled. "You'll have to tell me more about this export compliance job you have. I asked around. Most people have never heard of an export officer."

She appreciated his interest in her work. For a man who worked with his hands, he didn't seem to mind intelligent women. Her ex-husbands never wanted to talk about her career. They were more interested in the stock market, golf and sex. Even sex was about satisfying themselves.

She followed him into the kitchen. There was a setting for two, a fondue pot, cut vegetables, a bottle of wine, and a small plate with cubed cheese and bread.

Most men she dated never liked it.

She was very impressed.

"I love fondue. How did you know?"

"I guessed. I knew you weren't the Lou's Steakhouse type of woman."

They both laughed.

"I have something for you."

He left the room and brought back a dozen red roses and a box of chocolates. She was startled.

"Happy Valentine's day."

"For me? Thank you."

She accepted the candy and the flowers and laid them on the table. She didn't have any plans for Valentine's Day and helping April dress for the dance was the highlight of her evening.

Now Jack surprised her with wine, dinner and roses.

She wrapped her arms around his waist. She pressed her ear against his chest and heard the rhythmic beating of his heart. She tilted her head back and looked up at him.

His moustache lightly scratched the top of her lips. She didn't mind the new feeling.

It was the slowest and yet the fastest kiss that she'd ever had.

It took her a moment to come back into focus.

"You're welcome."

Other than the stoppage of the kiss, the pair stood motionless in the kitchen. Jack's arms were around her waist and he wasn't ready to let her go.

Not just yet.

"Do you want me to help with dinner?" She asked.

"Sure." He grinned. "You bring the meat out of the fridge and I'll start the pots."

"Will do."

***

"Well that was delicious." She said as she dipped her last marshmallow into the chocolate bowl. She sipped her third glass of wine and Jack was getting better looking by the minute.

"Yes, it was. I'm enjoying the company."

"You're not." She laughed. "All I've talked about is work, work, work."

He took the skewer from her and placed the marshmallow on her plate. He stuck his fork in it and offered her a bite.

"Oooh, sinful," she moaned as she savored the last bite. "And what was that wine? I couldn't quite place the vintage."

Jack laughed, "I'm sorry, Ms. Katie, but I picked that up at the grocery mart on the way home. I don't think it has a vintage."

Katie laughed again but this time a little harder. "My turn to feed you." Trying to hold her fork steady, she stuck her skewer in a piece of green apple and dipped it in the chocolate. He gently guided her and she didn't mind his rough hands around hers. She pulled off the chocolate covered piece and fed it to him.

"Open up." She placed the morsel on his tongue and felt his lips close against her fingers. His tongue swirled around her manicured nails.

She moaned.

She pulled out her fingers and reached for another piece of apple.

"This time we share."

She dipped the piece into the chocolate and fed it to him. He opened his mouth and closed his lips over half of the apple. She placed her lips on the other end kissing him and sectioned off her piece to chew.

"Sinful"

She wrapped her arms around his neck and kissed him. His arms wrapped around her back.

His tongue swirled around hers.

Her tongue tasted the chocolate on his.

The nine chimes of the kitchen clock brought each of them back to reality. They were still engrossed in their passion for each other.

"Well that was lovely, Mr. Jack."

"I agree. It was, Miss Katie."

"I'd like to try that again." She pulled his neck towards her and pressed her lips against his.

A few moments later, he brushed her hair from her face and whispered in her ear. "Let's go to the living room. I'll bring another bottle of wine."

She reclined on the couch in front of the TV. He brought two glasses along with the bottle of Chardonnay he'd opened in the kitchen. She got comfortable and snuggled with him. For the first time in her life, she felt secure. Nothing or no one was ever going to hurt her again and he was going to make sure of it.

Jack turned on the movie that they agreed to watch together. Five minutes into the movie, she was fast asleep.

An hour and a half later, she woke up.

"What time is it?"

"Ten-thirty." He answered and released her so she could sit up straight.

Her eyebrows crinkled and she looked around the room to assess her whereabouts. "It's time for me to go home. I'll turn into a pumpkin if I'm not out of here."

"You can't drive yet. You had too much wine at dinner. I'll get the guestroom ready."

"Here?" She said in a half-groggy surprise.

"Yes, here. Let me help you up the stairs."

"No," she protested, "it's fine. I can go home."

"No DUI's on my watch. You're staying here in the guest room."

She nodded in agreement and allowed him to help her up the stairs. She sat on the side of the bed and didn't' notice that he left. He returned and brought her his pajamas to wear.

"I can't change. You have to change me," she said seductively.

"No, ma'am. I'm not taking a piece of clothing off your body. You're drunk and I've watched those shows on the TV before; I'm not ending up on one of them," he said vehemently.

"Fine, then I'll change you."

She stood up to confront him. She placed her hand in the middle of his chest and felt the throbbing of his heart just like the time in front of the house.

She popped one button at a time on his shirt, down past his navel to the top of his belt buckle.

He stood there motionless as her pink manicured fingernails explored his long thick chest hair. She unzipped his pants and reached through the opening and stroked his erection. He removed his belt and she unbuttoned his trousers.

His pants and boxers dropped to the floor.

She pulled him closer, placed her lips to his earlobe and nipped lightly.

He couldn't resist her.

Nor did he want to.

"Okay, you win. I'll change you."

He moaned at the sensation of her touch caressing his balls, and enwrapping her fingers around his shaft. Sweat beaded on his forehead and the muscles tightened in his thighs. The more she stroked him the stiffer his erection became.

She lowered her head and downed his penis between her lips. He grasped a clump of her hair and bobbed it in a rhythmic motion over it. The sensation of her tongue rolling over him aroused the deep passion within his loins.

His calves tightened and his eyes rolled upward. His body quivered. He lifted her head and released his climax.

He pulled her to her feet. He moistened his lips and covered hers breathing his desire into her. She wrapped her arms around his back and squeezed his lower muscles.

He grazed his fingers over the skin beneath the hemline of her dress, felt the flush of her heat against his touch.

She stepped back, loosened her belt, and pulled her sweater dress over her head.

She shoved his shirt down his arms. It fell to the floor and landed around his ankles. He drew her in tight, snapped her bra with one hand and grasped her buttocks with the other. He laid her down on the bed. She parted her legs enough for him to rest comfortably between them.

He laid kisses between her breasts and ended them at the center of her navel. He lowered his head below her waist. He bit her candy apple red thong, tugged it away and slid his fingers inside her core.

She grabbed the back of his head and pushed his nose between her thighs.

He obliged her request.

She moaned as he breathed against her mound, her fingers tightening in his hair when he lapped at her pearl. The prickliness of his moustache tickled her with each movement of his lips.

She took short, shallow breaths but couldn't hold out long, lost herself to the pleasure of his kiss.

He raised his head and pulled himself above her. He pressed his lips against hers and guided his shaft between her thighs. He invaded her hollow with a gentle rocking motion.

He lifted his head and arched his back. Each thrust into her tightened every muscle in his body.

She wrapped her fingers around his biceps, curled her nails into his flesh, her body fluttering from her first orgasm, riding the wave to a second with the motions of his body within hers.

Her back arched.

Her lips opened on a silent scream as her legs tightened around his waist and he thrust once more against her, body braced within her heat.

They came together, the euphoria winking out the world around them until it was just his heavy chest lying against hers, the heat of her fingers tangling in his hair as she held him close.

He slowly pulled away from her and reclined on the bed at her side.

She shivered and curled deeper into his warmth while he pulled the blankets up around them.

He whispered in her ear as she drifted off to sleep. "Goodnight."

CHAPTER 11

Katie woke up Saturday morning with a throbbing headache and didn't recognize the room she was in. The daylight that beamed through the window was difficult to look at.

She knew she was naked and felt a warm body beside her. His arm was around her waist and she glided her fingers down his skin to his rough hand. She felt a twitch of a hairy moustache in the nape of her neck and heard the light snore as he breathed against her throat.

She rolled over to see.

Jack.

He didn't appear to have any clothes on either.

She remembered making love to him but thought she'd dreamed it.

Guess not.

She was too busy to start dating again. Her career was all she had and for the past week, she'd stepped away from it to spend a lot of time with the Williams' family.

***

Jack held her close during the night and thought about the events that led up to last night. He and the girls agreed not to tell Katie about dinner and he knew that it was a big gamble in the sense that she might have already had plans. Making love to her wasn't part of the plan but he didn't mind the unexpected close of the evening.

He opened his eyes and looked into hers.

She asked, "What happened last night? The last thing I remember you said I couldn't go home and you were getting the guestroom ready."

"I brought you my pajamas. You asked me to change you. I declined. You undressed me. Do I need to tell you the rest?"

"Oh…I thought I dreamed that. I didn't mean to throw myself at you. Why didn't you stop me?" She pulled the covers closer.

"You were pretty persistent and you weren't taking no for an answer." He reached for his pajama top and handed it to her.

She quickly put it on. "Where are the girls? They can't find me here in your bed."

"The girls are still with friends. I'll get up and make you some coffee."

She watched as he got out of bed. He had a strong muscular back and thick legs.

How could she not remember making love to all of that?

He turned, looked at her briefly and closed the door behind him.

She took a deep breath and pulled his pajama top closer around her. It was extremely large on her. When she stood up, it reached mid-thigh and wore like a nightgown.

She gathered her clothes and washed up in the bathroom down the hall. She assumed it was the one shared by the girls, as it was pink with ballerinas on the wall. She tried to fix her makeup as best as she could.

Thirty minutes later, she smelled the aroma of bacon cooking. Her stomach growled and she had to admit that she was getting a little hungry. She went downstairs and entered the kitchen. He had breakfast prepared. She took a seat at the table and he brought her a cup of coffee and food.

"This is a pretty large plate. I can't eat all of this."

He served her bacon, eggs, biscuits and grits.

It was more than enough breakfast and calories for the day.

"The girls aren't here. You could use a little weight. Try to eat what you can." He sat next to her with a similar plate of food.

"I won't allow myself to get fat." She protested.

"That's good. I won't allow you to be undernourished." He said in a matter-of-fact tone. He buttered his biscuit and watched to see if she would eat.

"Your girls can't find out about this." She forked a few bites of the eggs.

"Too late. They're the ones that set this up." He gave her a half-crooked smile and was pleased at releasing the secret plan.

"What?" She exclaimed.

"The girls and Mrs. Simmons helped set up the fondue. Mrs. Simmons taught me how to work the pot."

"Those little matchmakers. So, they both stayed with friends on purpose."

He snickered, "Most likely."

She couldn't get mad. She was pleased with the fact that the girls liked her so well. "I really have to go. I didn't check my calendar."

"Finish your breakfast first." He ordered. "You had quite a bit to drink last night. You need your strength."

She was in a no-win argument. Breakfast was tasty and so was the company but it didn't ease her concerns. "What are you going to tell your daughters?"

"What do you want me to tell them?"

She blushed profusely, "Certainly nothing about us doing, you know." She lifted her hand and twirled the end strands of her hair. "You can tell them we had a nice time talking over dinner. Don't give them any false expectations."

"Yes, ma'am."

CHAPTER 12

Jack retrieved the girls early from their respective slumber parties. He reclined on the couch in the living room and May watched a cartoon on TV. Footsteps bounded down the stairs. April stood in front of him.

"How did everything go last night?" She asked.

He lifted his head and met her gaze. His response was noncommittal and unemotional. "Fine, April."

She was not to be deterred. She placed her hands on her hips, sucked in her chest, and blurted out, "Are you going to see her again?"

He sighed, "April, let it rest."

Her lips pursed and throat muscles tightened. "What's wrong with you? Just ask her out again."

Exasperated, he loosened his grip on the remote control in his hand. "It isn't that simple."

"You're making it complicated, Dad."

He stood up from the couch and looked down at his daughter. She was angry but he wasn't letting her control his life. He remained cool and firmed up his response. "April, I said let it rest. There is no more to discuss."

April threw up her hands and voiced her frustrations. "You're impossible." She stormed off to her room and stomped on each stair on the climb up.

***

Katie rushed out of the Williams' household to get home, take a long shower, and prepare for the day.

She couldn't believe her behavior last night.

Although Jack was an attractive man, he wasn't in her social class.

Making love to him wasn't in her plan.

After toweling off, she checked her planner. She'd missed her appointment with Mario but she still had time to put in a few early hours to play racquetball before going to a theater performance with her French group. She called her friend Donna to see if she was free.

Donna's phone started ringing and Katie impatiently paced the floor.

"Kaitlin, how are you?" the chipper voice said on the other end of the line. "I was just thinking about you."

Katie laughed.

It was a nickname her mother called her when she was little. Donna was one of the few that she allowed to call her that. She liked the way her southern drawl dragged out the "a" in her name.

Donna was well liked at Dupree. Her husband was a dentist and a specialist in restoration work. She worked part-time at a charity during the week while the kids were in school. "Can you meet for racquetball in an hour?"

"Sure, I was headed that way. Let's do lunch afterwards."

***

"Well that was a workout." Katie exclaimed as she sat across from Donna in the dining room at Dupree Country Club eating her tuna salad. "I'm tired of letting you win."

Donna grinned, "It isn't easy beating you and the last game was close. I'm slipping."

"How's the family?" Katie asked.

"Joe's doing fine, both kids are in school and you won't believe it, but I'm pregnant. Hopefully this is the last one." Donna sipped her mint flavored iced tea.

Katie almost choked on her tuna salad. She was sensitive to pregnancy news since the divorce. Unlike her ex-husbands, Donna's husband was very attentive to his family. She was one of the lucky ones.

Katie forced a smile on her face. "Congratulations."

"Thank you. Joe will have to cut back on his golf game when the baby is born. When he or she gets a little bigger, we'll need more help with getting the kids to activities. How's everything with you? Meet anyone interesting lately?"

"I actually did at Doug's wedding. I've spent a lot of time with the Williams' family. April is a soccer player, May is a chef, and their father, Jack, is a landscaper."

"Where's his wife, girlfriend, or significant other?"

"Widowed."

Donna's eyes sparked with excitement, "Widowed! How old is he? What happened?"

Katie took in a deep breath and reflected on her brief conversations with Jack. She'd never asked him about what happened and only noticed the sad faraway look in his eyes when his late wife was mentioned. The girls mentioned her in passing and she only knew her name was Paige because it was on a refrigerator magnet in the kitchen.

"He didn't say." She said solemnly and drifted back in thought about him and his family. She realized that she didn't know what to do with Jack and knew very little about his life.

Donna stuck her fork in her salad and scrapped off the bacon and cheese. Katie wondered why she didn't just ask them to remove it from the salad before it was served.

"Find out."

Find out? The thought had never crossed her mind to get to know Jack beyond light conversation.

Donna dabbed the dressing off her lips. "It must be hard for a man to raise kids alone, especially being widowed."

Katie thought about her dad.

He'd had to do the same thing as Jack, raise kids without a mother. It hadn't dawned on her until that moment how awful it must have been for him to lose someone so dear to him unexpectedly and forever.

She'd been a spoiled brat anytime he tried to bring someone home to meet her.

And she'd been a spoiled brat about his relationships ever since.

CHAPTER 13

"No, let me do it."

"You can't. You're too small."

"Mrs. Simmons taught me. I know what I'm doing."

Jack woke up from his sleep and overheard the argument from his kids downstairs. He slid his legs over the side of his bed and put his head in his hands. He'd had a few beers the night before after the kids went to bed. Now they were up early and making him pay for it.

He walked down the stairs and entered the kitchen to witness the argument that was continuing in louder and louder decibels.

"What's going on?" He growled. "I can't sleep through this."

April's anger turned towards him. "You should be up anyway. May is trying to cook on the stove and I'm telling her she's too short and she's insisting that she can do this."

May shoved her sister and ran to hug her dad. "I can cook. I'm making pancakes. Mrs. Simmons taught me and Sissy won't let me."

"She's gonna burn the house down!"

"No, I won't," May snapped back. "You're just mad because you don't know how to do it. Mommy always let me help."

Jack's rubbed his bleary eyes and tried to focus on the drama unfolding in front of him. "Can't you both work together?"

"Can't you do something besides drinking and sleeping? I have practice in an hour and you're just now getting up. This family has to continue and you have to be a part of it."

"April! Watch that tone of voice." He said with a note of firmness.

April crossed her arms and huffed. "Yes, sir. I haven't eaten yet and you know how long it takes to get to the field. Please get dressed. I'll handle this."

Jack was stuck between the girls and wasn't clear on whose side to take. He came up with a solution.

"April, let May cook and help her. I'll get dressed so you won't be late to soccer practice."

"Fine," April huffed.

***

April pressed her finger against her passenger side window. "Look over to the right. That's Katie's house."

Jack glanced over to see the large lawn with more of the grass dead than alive. It was a brick home with lots of windows. He passed through this elite subdivision often.

"Can we stop?" April asked. She turned and smiled at him.

"No." He sped up a little. "You'll be late to practice."

She reached behind her head and tightened her band on her ponytail. "You're staying for practice, aren't you?"

"Yes." He stared through the windshield and pressed the brake for the upcoming four-way stop sign.

"Don't sit in the car. Come watch me." She pulled her shin guards out of her duffel bag and strapped them on her legs.

"I will, April."

Eighteen. I'm waiting for eighteen.

He pulled into the parking lot at the field.

She opened the door and faced him before she left the car. "You're working late next week. Call her to see if she'll take me to practice."

April's cleats hit the ground and she snatched her backpack from the floor of the car. Before he could answer, she slammed the car door shut.

"That damn teenager is going to be the death of me," he grumbled and stared at his cell phone.

Katie appeared to be a busy woman and didn't have time to play mommy to his daughters.

But April was right.

He was working late next week she would be late to practice by the time he got home.

He reached in his back pocket for his wallet and pulled out her card.

Katie Pennington Leigh
Director, Export Compliance
Parker Logistics

He looked at his watch. It was almost 7:00 p.m. and he was sure she wouldn't be in her office. He could leave a message and that would satisfy April's demand.

He fully expected a voicemail but he got Katie instead.

"Export Compliance, Katie speaking."

"Uh," he stammered, "It's Jack." He leaned back in his seat and gripped the phone tight."

"How are you? How's the family?"

"Fine." He answered and opened the door to stand up. He leaned against the car and looked over to the field to try and see April practicing.

"What can I do for you?"

"I need a favor. I'm working late next week. April needs a ride to practice. Are you available to take her?"

"Hmm. What days and what time?"

"Monday and Wednesday. Practice starts at seven." He folded his arms across his chest and expected a negative response.

"Sure, I'll take her." She said cheerfully.

Perplexed, Jack wasn't sure about what he heard. "You will?"

"Of course. I'm clearing off my calendar so I can do this."

"Thank you. Just so you are aware, you'll be expected to stay for dinner afterwards. It's the least I can do since you are doing me and my family a favor."

"Maybe." She laughed nervously. "I still have a lot of work to do and will need to get up to go to work in the morning. Let's see what happens."

He nodded. "Yes, ma'am. I'll see you next week."

CHAPTER 14

Katie shoved her work in her briefcase and looked at her watch. She had forty-five minutes to arrive at April's house and take her to practice. She quickly rushed out of the office.

When she pulled in the driveway, April was outside waiting. Katie rolled down the window.

"Hi Katie, I'm glad you're here." April walked to the passenger side of the car.

Katie was glad she picked up a new strawberry scented air freshener. Soccer gear was quite odorous. She'd made it a point to open up two air fresheners before picking up April.

April tossed her soccer bag in the backseat. She dropped her dirty cleats on the floorboard in the front passenger side.

The dry dust exploded all over the floorboard.

"I'm sorry. I'm ruining your car."

"That's ok. I'll have it washed. I'm going to find some things to cover the floor and the seats so you can be comfortable."

"Thanks for taking me to soccer practice."

"You're welcome."

"Can I ask you something?"

"Sure."

"What do you think of my dad?"

Katie glanced over at her with a puzzled expression and continued to drive to the field. "I'm not sure what you're asking me."

"I mean would you go out with him again?"

Again?

Another date?

"Your father and I are very different. We don't have a lot in common."

"So, you wouldn't go out with him again."

"I didn't say that."

April sighed, "You're just as impossible as he is."

***

While sitting at soccer practice and waiting for April to finish, she thought about calling her dad. She'd put it off long enough.

It was time to reconcile.

"Daddy, it's me." She said when Don picked up the phone.

"I've tried to call you all week. I was beginning to worry about you."

"I know, Dad." She sniffled and stifled back the tears, "I'm sorry. I know it must have been hard to lose Mom. I only thought of myself. I think I understand better now."

After all these years, she still grieved the loss of her mother in ways she couldn't express to anyone. She avoided looking at mothers with their daughters for afternoon tea, prom dresses, and family holidays. After she knew that her mother was never coming back, her heart ached for a very long time.

"I'm sorry too, Tiger. This old man knows that he can never replace your mom."

Her stifled tears overflowed and rolled down her cheeks. "I'll call you later. Let's get together this week. I love you."

"I love you too."

***

She composed herself and walked toward the field. Vanessa waved for her to come sit with her on the bleachers. She was the mother of the goalie, Audra. Vanessa had dark brown hair and was six feet tall. Her daughter was 5'10" and going to be even taller when she finished her growth spurt. This time Katie had her seat cushion in hand.

"Hi Katie. I'm glad you're back."

"It's great to see you." She smiled and took a seat beside her on the bleachers. Vanessa was the leader of the team gossip column.

"I know you aren't involved in team news, but we're getting a new forward next year. Tracy wasn't happy with her playing time so after this season she's moving on."

"Oh my," Katie responded. Although she didn't have much to add, she never imagined that youth soccer would be a big networking event. In the few practices and games she'd attended, she'd met VP's of banks, doctors, lawyers, executives and even a sports team owner. She'd also met homemakers, artists, writers, and record producers.

"So how are you and Jack getting along? I was surprised when you came to the game and sat with him. He usually keeps to himself since Paige died. No one knew he was dating again."

Katie sat up straighter and looked Vanessa in the eyes. She'd only been to one soccer game and a couple of practices. She wasn't expecting that everyone would assume that she and Jack were a couple. She wondered how much the team suspected. "I'm just a friend of the family. I met April and Jack at Doug and Lisa's wedding. Were you there?"

"Yes, I was. I'm sorry to make assumptions. The team has been concerned about the family. Jack and April both looked happy when you came to the game. He's been grieving for a long time."

Katie nodded and returned to her thoughts. How dreadful it must have been for him. She only found her husbands in bed with other women. What if she found them dead? Although it may have been preferable at the time, how would she have handled it?

***

Katie and April arrived at the Williams' household.

This time, the aroma of fried chicken wafted through the air.

When they entered the kitchen, Jack turned and waved. He continued to remain focused on frying the chicken. May stood at the table and stirred the batter for the waffles.

He grabbed a dishrag and wiped his hands. He smiled and winked at Katie. "Staying for dinner?"

She hesitated before responding. "Well…" She had a pile of work to do and planned to go home to finish it. "Okay, but I can't stay late."

"Awesome!" April cheered. "I'll go change." She left the kitchen and ran upstairs.

May washed her hands and wiped them on the yellow and white hand towel. She wore a light blue apron with a rooster in the middle. She came over and hugged Katie. "I was hoping you would stay."

Katie welcomed her affection. She looked up at Jack and said, "I suppose you want a hug too."

"Yes, ma'am. I'm not turning that down."

May darted out of the kitchen, ran up the stairs, and shouted: "Sissy! It's on the table."

He opened his arms and she wrapped hers around the middle of his back. He lowered his head and brushed his face against hers. He caught a whiff of her light floral scented perfume. Her soft cheek brushed smoothly against his clean-shaven one.

She turned her head enough that she could place a soft kiss under his moustache.

Two sets of footsteps bounded down the stairs. She loosened her arms and took a step backward. He opened his eyes and released his hold.

They gazed into each other's eyes until the silence was broken.

"Should I get the condiments?" April asked.

"Sure." He answered slowly.

Katie inhaled and coughed lightly. She exhaled to release the building sexual tension between her and Jack. "Well, I'm ready for dinner. Is there anything I need to do?"

"Yep. Silence your phone for twenty minutes. I'm sure the work will be there. We would like to spend some time with you and not compete with your office."

Silence my phone?

She looked around her. The girls bustled around the kitchen and prepared the place setting for the family meal. Jack placed the chicken in a serving dish and set it on the table.

She didn't know what to do. She mostly ate alone. If she traveled, she ate alone. Since the divorce, she ate alone at home. If she went out, she ate with business associates or friends but not at home. This was a new experience. Family dining.

When everyone was finished, the family took his or her seat at the table and motioned for her to sit. She took a chair and picked up her purse. She pulled out her phone and stared at it.

Twenty minutes

No calls.

Off it was.

CHAPTER 15

It was Thursday evening when Jack stopped by the store and picked up a six-pack of beer. He realized he hadn't drank much beer since Katie became a frequent guest. She was a "wine connoisseur." He made sure to stock her favorite chardonnay in the refrigerator.

He sectioned a piece of last night's lasagna and heated it in the microwave.

My baby is taking care of her daddy.

Tomorrow's lunch was in a Tupperware dish ready for him to grab and go. He was thankful that May took over the kitchen. She saved him a lot of time and money in lunch and he really appreciated her effort.

April and May were both in their respective rooms when he popped the lid off an ice-cold brew to compliment his lasagna that was piping hot out of the microwave. He almost left it in too long and the strong scent of oregano and thyme filled the air.

Just as he was about to enter the living room, April rushed in the kitchen.

"Your turn to call her." She demanded.

"April!" He shouted. "Will you leave that woman alone?"

She crossed her arms and didn't budge from her floor space. She stared him directly in the eyes.

"Now!" She demanded. "Invite her to family movie night."

"She's got a full calendar. You heard her. She works a lot."

April snatched the phone from the receiver and handed it to him.

He wasn't prepared for a showdown over a woman he just met and was very reluctant to "push his luck" beyond the one night stand they'd had together. She never really expressed an interest in dating him beyond their encounter on Valentine's Day.

Still, he accepted the phone and dialed Katie's number.

***

Katie was home working on papers from the office. She took a break in the kitchen and looked in her nearly empty cabinet and refrigerator.

She'd spent more time at the Williams' than she had at home lately.

April and May told her all about school, practice, boys and any other topics of interest that were appropriate dinner conversation. She listened intently and was amazed at how much she had missed being a teenage girl.

She looked forward to the days that she had dinner with the family. It was a big difference to coming home to an empty house. The chatter and conversation of an extended family was a new experience.

When she was younger, she only had her dad for the day-to-day meals. After middle school, he worked late and missed many meals with her.

It was 8:30 p.m. when she made her second cup of coffee. She was fighting sleep and more tired than usual.

Normally, she had a lot of energy and stayed up very late. Her new life with the Williams' family must be taking its toll on her.

May prepared heavy meals and she wasn't used to the new diet.

The ringing phone interrupted her thoughts.

"Hi, Jack," She stretched out her arms and yawned. "How are you this evening?"

"Better than you. You sound tired."

She rubbed her eyes and tried to compose herself. "I'm awake. I swear. I have a lot of work to do. I can do this. I'm okay. How are you?" She became more incoherent with every tick of the clock.

He'd better talk fast because she wasn't going to make it.

"You already asked me that," he chuckled. "Check your calendar for tomorrow night. The girls want you to come here for movie night."

"Huh? Movie. What?" She picked up her planner. The symphony orchestra was playing and she had season tickets. The tickets were part of her settlement in the divorce. She normally gave them away at the office if she didn't have a date.

"Yep, I can go." She said in a groggy voice. Her face on top of her forearm as she talked to him and his voice drifted away.

"You don't sound good. Are you okay?"

"I'm sorry. I'm exhausted all of a sudden. Will you call me in the morning to confirm? I should be more alert then."

"No problem. Good night, Katie." He said.

"Good night, my love."

The phone went silent.

***

When Katie woke up in the wee hours of the morning, she found herself asleep on top of her work papers. She dragged herself to bed and only got a few more hours of sleep before she had to get up.

"You've got to be kidding me." She said when the alarm clock went off.

Dragging herself out of bed, she took her shower and got dressed for the day. Two cups of coffee last night didn't buy her the extra energy that she bargained for. She wanted to stay up late and finish reading the trade deal that she was going to review with clients in a conference call later in the day, but that just made for a hectic morning until the phone rang.

"Export Compliance, Katie speaking."

"It's Jack. Do you remember our conversation last night?"

Katie thought through the events of last night.

Coffee, paper work, sleep, movie.

Movie.

Yes. Movie.

"Of-of course I do. Something about a movie. Was it tomorrow?"

"It's tonight. Are you free to come by?"

"Yes, I am. My planner is up to date. I'll be there." She frantically searched the pages of her calendar. There was a note about Jack's movie night. She didn't remember marking it down but she'd thought she spoke to him last night.

She was concerned about her sleepiness and lax in memory. The calendar was her way of tracking her events, but that wasn't related to her difficulty with staying awake. She was going to do something that she never thought she would do. Slow down.

Scary thought for a workaholic.

Nevertheless, she had to keep this job.

It was all she had.

CHAPTER 16

Since Katie had forgotten about movie night, she left work early to rush home and change into comfortable attire.

Her routine was off.

Everything was moved around to accommodate a soccer schedule and dinner in the evenings. She'd missed her French club and Spanish Club meetings. She'd rescheduled her fitness activities. She'd even put off some corporate events unless they were impossible to move or she couldn't send one of her employees to attend.

She was on the road once again to the Williams' household. Her life had changed dramatically since the day Doug got married. She was now involved in the lives of the Williams' family.

She felt sorry for Jack and believed that he must miss Paige dearly. The girls sometimes mentioned her and it was a difficult conversation to have with them. It brought up the same feelings she had when her own mother died.

She'd never forget Twyla Jane Pennington.

She avoided the conversation about Paige with Jack because it seemed like he preferred not to talk about it. He seemed solemn at times when the girls would mention anything about her. Maybe it was still too painful for him and he wasn't ready to move on yet.

She arrived and he opened the door to welcome her into the house.

***

"So, have we decided on a pizza?" Katie asked. "Veggie is my preference."

"We'll get a couple of them. I like the meat lovers."

Well look at that.

He actually gave his opinion first before the girls. This is a rare occasion and she would mark it on her calendar.

"I only like cheese on my pizza," May chimed in.

"I'll eat any of it and pick off what I don't want," April said.

"Okay," Jack said. "I'll order three medium pizzas. Cheese, meat lovers, and veggie."

"I'll start the popcorn." April hopped up from the table and grabbed the seeds from the cabinet. May led Katie to the living room while Jack placed the order.

***

"My daddy usually sits on the corner and mommy always sat there next to daddy." May pointed to the empty spot on the brown leather couch and continued. "I sat under mommy, and sissy sat next to me."

Tears rolled from May's eyes. She grabbed Katie and hugged her tight. Katie sat down so she could hold her while she sobbed.

"It's okay to miss your mommy. I miss mine too." Katie said in a loving voice.

"But why did she have to go? Daddy won't talk to me about it. He just says it was her time."

Katie was rapidly thinking of something to say that would ease May's woes. This was her first conversation with someone so young about the death of a mother and this time it wasn't about her.

"She went to be with the Angels. God needed her home."

For someone who wasn't particularly religious, she wasn't sure where that came from.

"But why? I need her here."

Talking about death to a very young child was not in her field of expertise. It was tougher than a negotiation with an executive vice president on export compliance practices. She at least had knowledge on the subject and had many years of practice.

"She'll always be with you, sweetheart." Katie took May's hand and placed it in the center of May's light orange colored sweater. "Here."

Jack stood in the living room and overheard the conversation between the pair. It was amazing how a woman who didn't have kids of her own was able to talk to May and console her with no reservations.

He believed that Katie was more selfish than she expressed around his family. He was almost accustomed to her snobby attitude about clothing, wine, and coffee. The economic roast coffee wasn't good enough for her. Katie's beans must be handpicked personally by Juan Valdez.

All of that didn't matter.

He was falling in love with her anyway.

April appeared behind Jack and brought two large bowls of popcorn.

"It's ready." She called out as she walked over to the coffee table. "Lots of butter and light salt. Just how I like it."

April plopped on her end of the couch and May sat next to her while drying her eyes. April picked up the remote and started the movie. Jack sat in his usual spot and Katie sat next to him. Blankets were available for everyone.

Fifteen minutes into the movie, they paused it so Jack could answer the door for the pizza delivery.

They were halfway through the second movie when the pizzas were devoured and the leftovers were put away. All were engrossed in the movie. Jack's eyes softened as looked down the couch at the women in his life. Katie nestled next to him and he held her hand in his lap.

I love my family.

***

"I have to go." Katie said. The credits were rolling down the screen as she fought a yawn. "It's getting late."

Jack rose from the couch and offered his hand for her to stand. "The girls are asleep. I'll walk you to your car."

Katie delicately moved May to lay on her sister then accepted his hand and stood up. She looked back at the girls.

They're adorable.

"The guest room is ready if you want it. You're welcome to stay."

She picked up her purse and walked over to the door. "No. I have a lot to do tomorrow."

"Alright."

He followed her to her car and she fidgeted with her keys, not sure what all she wanted to do, not sure she wanted to really leave.

She raised her gaze to his, "Goodnight."

"Goodnight. The offer still stands."

"Not this time."

"Thank you for talking with May about Paige. It's been difficult to explain it to her. It's been tough for all of us."

Katrina's voice echoed in her head: *Find out.*

"Do you mind if I ask you something?"

"Go ahead."

"How did your wife pass away?"

He took a deep breath and let it go slowly. "Blood clot to the brain. My lawyer thinks it was caused by a medication that she was taking for a chest cold."

Katie's eyes moistened as she looked into his eyes. She held her breath and let it out slowly. She loosened her clutch on the door handle of the car.

He continued. "I called from work to check up on her and she sounded worse than when I left her that morning. I insisted on coming home to take her to the doctor. By the time I got here, she was still in bed and I couldn't wake her. I called 911 and rode in the ambulance with her. They didn't call it until we got to the hospital but she was... She never woke up to say goodbye."

Katie forced herself to breathe, to process, to reach out and cup his cheek, shift so she could pull him into a hug, hold him close so he couldn't see her tears at the pain she saw in his eyes. "I'm so sorry for your loss."

"Thank you."

She tipped her head back, but he only kissed her forehead.

CHAPTER 17

"What time is it?" Katie rolled over to see the alarm clock. "Ten! I overslept."

She jumped out of bed and grabbed her pink bathrobe. Her aerobics class started at 9:30 a.m. and she'd missed most of it.

"Why the hell can't I get up anymore? What happened to my alarm?" She picked up the clock and noticed that the alarm wasn't set.

She looked out of her bedroom and saw Jack's truck parked at the end of her driveway.

"What the hell is he doing here?" She stomped out of her room, down the stairs, out of the door and down the driveway.

Her mailbox was missing.

Several bricks were on the ground and a mixture of cement was close by. Jack was on his knees and building something, his back to her as she growled walking towards him.

"What are you doing?" she demanded.

Jack jerked at her approach, but smiled when she came near enough. "Replacing your mailbox."

"I didn't ask you to do that," she shouted. "I didn't hire you to do that!"

He shrugged, wiped the sweat off his brow. "It's not a big deal, and it was the least I could do with all your help with the girls." He grinned, "Nice curlers, by the way."

"What?" She screamed.

"They match your bathrobe. Do you always sleep naked?"

She snarled, lips moving but not sure what to say. "I'm going back into the house." She tightened the belt on her bathrobe and marched back up the driveway.

He snickered, and turned back to the mailbox as she slammed her front door.

***

Katie showered and pulled out her light blue jogging suit. Her spandex shorts were too tight and the joggers allowed her more room to expand. Her weight was an issue and she didn't know how to control it.

"Maybe I'm just getting old."

She sat down in the breakfast room with her fresh brewed coffee in hand. She looked out of the window and into the backyard. Jack was standing by her pond.

"What the hell is he doing now?"

She put down her coffee, slipped her feet into her flip-flops and walked outside.

Water was flowing from the fountain!

He faced her with his arms folded. She approached and stood next to him. "Mr. Williams, I didn't hire you as my personal handyman."

He glanced down at her. "Your pump's fixed."

"Clearly."

"I don't have the tools with me, but I'll come back and fix your porch swing."

"You don't have to do that."

"You didn't have to take my daughter to soccer, but you did. Thank you. I really appreciate you."

She nodded, pursed her lips and tried not to smile. It was nice to have someone take care of these things for her. He ex-husband, Richard was useless when it came to being handy.

She turned up her eyes and released the smile she was holding back. "You're welcome."

"Dinner."

"Dinner?" She asked.

"Tonight." He said in a steady, low-pitched voice.

They both turned toward each other. Her gaze met his.

Sweat from the heat slid down his forehead.

She felt a rise in the temperature but it wasn't from the Georgia sun.

"Is this how you ask a woman out?" She folded her arms across her chest.

"Forgive me, ma'am. It's been a while. I've got no game left when it comes to asking a woman out."

He wiped his brow with the back of his hand.

His T-shirt was drenched from the work he'd done that morning.

How could she say no to his simple request?

"Yes."

His eyes widened with surprise. "You haven't checked your calendar."

"I know what's on my calendar today. Six o'clock p.m. sharp and don't be late." She turned her back and marched across the grass to her house.

"Katie."

She stopped and turned around to face him.

"Three o'clock. We'll have dinner around six."

She folded her arms and scowled. "I haven't checked my calendar."

He nodded. "I know. Call me and let me know if three is good for you."

Her mouth curled upward and her lips were pressed tight. The harder she tried to refrain from smiling, the more she blushed. "I'll let you know."

She turned her head before he could see the rest of the smile that escaped her lips and widened across her face.

***

Jack was thankful that the girls had slumber parties that evening. He dropped them off after lunch and didn't divulge his evening plans. They would have false expectations, and April would grill him constantly on Katie if he mentioned her or the state of their relationship, if he could call it that.

Dinner had seemed like a good idea when he mentioned it to Katie.

The mere fact that she agreed to go was a little surprising.

At one-thirty, not having heard from her, he called to confirm.

"This is Katie."

"It's Jack." He heard loud pop music in the background, which soon faded. "Sounds like you're at a party."

She laughed. "Just a little exercise. Are we still on at three?"

"Yes, ma'am."

"What's the attire?"

"Very casual. Whatever you're comfortable in."

She sighed with a laugh, "I hope you're not taking me to fast food."

He chuckled. "I know better than that. I'd fix you leftovers from May's cooking before I'd suggest that, and May's cooking is like eating at a five-star restaurant. Hmm, now that I think of it. She did make some pretty good Chilean sea bass—"

"I'm in," she interrupted. "Casual it is."

"I've got somewhere I'd like to take you before dinner. So, I'll see you at three. Bye."

"Bye."

***

It was 2:45 p.m. when Jack arrived at Katie's home. He pulled in the driveway and glanced over at her newly built brick mailbox. He was thankful that his Uncle Eddy had taught him how to lay bricks years ago.

He parked the car in her driveway and walked to the front door with a small box in hand. He knew he was a little early and she might not be ready. Pushing the doorbell, he waited for an answer.

She opened the door dressed in a multi-colored paisley dress with her hair pulled back in a ponytail. He looked down at her red open toed sandals then tilted his head up to look into her sparkling green eyes.

"Welcome." She grinned at his stare. "Is this casual enough?"

"We're gonna do a lot of walking, so up to you."

"I'll bring my sneakers." She stepped back from the door and allowed him to come in.

He stepped in the foyer and handed her the box. "For you."

"Thank you." She crinkled her eyes and looked down at the gift. She lifted the lid and gasped. "Ew."

He laughed. "I take it you don't get a couple of caterpillars every day."

She opened the lid more carefully and looked at the critter-crawlers inside the box. "Not funny."

"It wasn't meant to be. I took a risk in bringing you these. They're not just any caterpillar, they're kings. They'll turn into monarch butterflies once they go through metamorphosis."

"And what am I supposed to do with them?" she asked unimpressed with this very unusual gift. She motioned for him to follow her to the kitchen where they both sat down at the table.

After they settled in their chairs, he answered her question.

"Watch them turn into butterflies. When I was a kid, my grandma loved butterflies so she got us monarchs every year for Easter. The Easter bunny would come with a basket and grandma would come to visit for dinner and bring my brother, sister, and myself a caterpillar. I used to make them give me theirs because they wouldn't take care of them. I looked forward to that every Easter. April and May both have their caterpillars. I make sure they get a few every year."

Katie smiled and lifted the lid off the box again. The tiny creatures were a tad creepy with their wiggling legs, but they never stopped munching on the plants lining the bottom of the case, and they were, kind of, cute, once she got past the bug part.

"These two will get together and make baby caterpillars. I've named them Katie and Jack." He winked at her.

She couldn't help but laugh.

He lifted the sleeve of the polo on his right arm. Katie walked around the table so she could get a closer look at his tattoo, the monarch with "Louann" inscribed underneath it.

"That's my grandma. I loved her dearly and I'll never forget her. There are five generations of Louann's. My grandmother's mom, my grandmother, my mom, my sister, and her daughter."

"That's a lot of Louann's." She chuckled.

"You have no idea. They wanted April or May to be named like them but Paige said no."

CHAPTER 18

Katie followed Jack to the pewter colored SUV in her driveway.

"Is this new?" She asked.

"Yes, ma'am."

"What happened to the van?"

"Traded it. I bought it a few days ago and it was ready to pick up today."

He reached for the handle and opened the door for her. She settled in the passenger side.

He walked around the car and got into the driver's side. He looked over at her.

"You look nice."

Katie laughed. "Nice! Do you know how long it took me to apply makeup and all I get is nice?"

He stuck his key in the ignition. "Yes ma'am. Nice." He looked out of the windshield and the SUV moved to the end of the driveway.

Katie shrugged her shoulders and looked at him. "Is that it?"

"No, ma'am. Do you like trains?"

Trains?

First, the one word to ask me out for dinner, then he tells me I look nice and now he's asking me about trains. Why did I agree to go out with this simple man?

"I guess so. Why?"

"We're going to Stone Mountain. Have you been there before?"

"No, I haven't."

"You're in for a treat."

Her cell phone rang.

"It's the office." Katie fumbled through her purse to find her phone.

"On a Saturday afternoon?" He asked.

"I have to take this call." She found it and answered. "Yes, Katrina."

Jack shook his head and continued to drive to Stone Mountain. She chatted for about ten minutes then finished her conversation.

"I'm sorry about that. I have clients coming in next week. I must attend to a few last-minute details. Don't worry, I'll do it tomorrow."

"We're here."

***

The train moved slowly down the tracks. It was an open-air rail car and a cool day. The trees were beginning to grow leaves and the grass was still more brown than green.

Katie had worn a sweater but didn't anticipate how cold it would be. She pulled her sleeves and hugged herself to get warm.

"Cold?" He took off his light jacket and wrapped it around her before she could answer.

"Uh yes, thank you." Having his jacket on reminded her of the time when she woke up in his bed. It was comforting. She relaxed her head on his shoulder and he wrapped his arm around her.

"Better."

She looked up him and smiled. "Yes."

"This is one of my favorite things to do. I love riding trains."

"I can't remember the last time I was on a train."

"April's mother worked for a train station. The three of us took a lot of trips before the divorce."

"You're divorced? I thought you were widowed." She looked up at Jack with curiosity about this revelation.

"I'm divorced and widowed. April and May have different mothers."

"I see." She said and looked out of the window at the passing trees and scenery.

"Have you been married before?" He asked.

She answered, "Yes, twice and it's not open for discussion."

"Yes, ma'am. Why ruin a perfectly great evening talking about ex-husbands? I'm sure they didn't appreciate you."

Wow.

He made up for the "nice" comment.

"They didn't. I want a man who values the work I do and fits into my social circle." She noticed the train slowed down as it climbed the side of the mountain.

"And that's hard to find?" He teased.

"Yes." She said. "Impossible. What are you looking for?"

"Who says I'm looking?"

She laughed. "Everyone looks."

"Alright." He nodded and smiled. "I want the same thing. Her social circle or where she works doesn't matter to me. She could work at the Piggly Wiggly as long as she loves me."

She pulled his jacket tighter around her arms to ward off the cold shiver that crept through her veins. "Well that should be simple enough. Maybe you can find Ms. Right in the cereal aisle."

He laughed and hugged her closer. "No, ma'am. Usually those women are there to feed families. It's difficult to meet single women when you are a single dad with kids, especially when one is a teenager."

"Is that why April asked me to meet you?"

"Yes." He said exasperated with his teenager's antics. "She wants me to date but only someone she picks. It took a while for me to get used to dating anyone after Paige died. I lost my best friend and talking to any woman was unnatural."

"I'm sure it's difficult for you. I have so much to do for work; I don't have time to meet anyone new."

He took his free hand and slid it under the palm of her hand. He looked down at her maroon colored acrylic nails on her ringless fingers. Her eyes followed his gaze to her fingers. He gave her hand a light squeeze.

"You'll meet the man you need."

***

"Are you hungry?" Jack asked while they were walking back to the SUV. He held Katie's hand and she took several quick steps to keep up with him.

"Yes, I'm starved." She panted. "I can usually keep pace but you're pretty fast."

He slowed down and moderated his pace. "I know where we can find the best Southern cuisine in the state of Georgia."

"Really?" Her eyes perked up. She had home cooked meals over the last few weeks and was accustomed to the change from her diet of low fat and raw vegetables. Unfortunately, her clothes weren't expanding to match the new diet.

"Sure. It'll take us thirty minutes to get there if traffic is kind to us."

"Okay."

Thirty minutes later, they pulled into the driveway of a rural neighborhood in Conyers. The truck in the driveway was similar to Jack's. It had "Williams Landscaping" painted on the side. He parked in next to it.

"Where are we?" She asked.

"My Mom and Dad's house." He grinned.

"Your parents! But why—"

Before Katie could finish her sentence, he got out of the SUV and was standing at her door to assist her to get out.

"Are they expecting us?"

His face beamed with pride. "Yes, ma'am. They are."

They walked up the steps to the wrap around porch. He rang the doorbell and it opened after the second ring.

"Mom." He leaned over and hugged the short thick woman with dark brown hair. She stood on her tiptoes and squeezed him.

"Is this Katie?" She asked and released him.

"Yes, it is."

Katie had a smile plastered on her face. She felt a little awkward with the fact that she was having dinner with his parents. Surprise dinners must be big in his family.

"How are you?" Katie extended her hand. She was met with a big hug from his mother instead.

"I'm so glad to meet you. My granddaughters have talked so much about you."

"This is my mother, Louann."

"You can call me Lu-Lu. My husband Tyler is in the yard out back. I'll have him come in to meet you.

"Tyler, Tyler!" She yelled and walked to the back of the house. She was soon outside and out of sight.

"I hope you don't mind." Jack said. "The girls talk about you a lot to my mom so she really wanted to meet you."

Katie's lips parted. She didn't know what to say. She couldn't decide whether she was angry or flattered. Angry because he didn't tell her in advance that she was meeting his mother and it appeared that everyone knew she was coming. Flattered because everyone seemed to be excited that she was here.

"I-I-I'm fine with this." She caught the aroma of cooked peaches mixed with the smell of a wood burning fire. Her hunger pangs were too noisy to ignore.

"This is Katie." Lu-Lu said. She returned with a man around the same height as Jack. His dark hair had strands of grey. He was a tall slender man with a similar frame as Jack's.

"Pleased to meet you." He extended his hand and she accepted. "I know you're hungry and the food's almost ready. Come out back."

Katie and Jack followed the pair to an enclosed porch on the back of the house. The red smoker was on the patio and Jack walked outside with his dad to attend to the food. Lu-Lu brought a few glasses to the table.

"Sweet tea." She offered and poured a glass for Katie before she could protest. She normally drank unsweet tea to watch her calories.

"Uh, thank you." She smiled and accepted the glass.

"I'll make your plate." Lu-Lu said.

"No." Jack said when he entered the room with a pan of smoked pork. "She's on a strict diet and I know you'll load her plate. I'll get it."

Katie protested. "I appreciate the offer but I can get my own plate thank you." She rose from the chair. "Please lead the way."

On the breakfast bar, there was an assortment of roast pork, fried chicken, baked beans, green bean casserole, cornbread and peach cobbler. She wasn't sure what she could eat from the cuisine and not stray from her diet. She chose to select small portions.

All four of them gathered at the table on the porch. Lu-Lu was the last one seated. She noticed the small portions on Katie's plate.

"Oh honey, there's plenty in there for you to eat. You don't have to be polite."

"Yes, thank you. This is plenty."

Jack interjected. "I'm taking her for ice-cream later. She's saving room for it."

Nice save. Katie lifted her fork and pushed the baked beans to the side of her plate.

"Jack says you work a lot and are really important at your job. It's a shame you're not married. You're such a pretty girl."

"Mom!" Jack exclaimed. "How's Aunt Chessie doing?"

Another save. That's two in a row. Katie smiled across the table at Lu-Lu.

"My son is widowed and available." Tyler said and winked at Katie. He turned to Lu-Lu and said, "I can't let you have all the fun."

"Tyler!" She laughed. "This is the first woman he's brought here since Paige passed. Show some respect."

Katie threw her head back and chuckled. His parents were a handful.

"Mom. Dad. I'm still at the table and so is Katie. Can you be like normal people and talk about their kids behind their backs."

"I've got cute baby pictures of him. I'll show you those the next time you come by."

"No, Mom. She's not interested."

Katie lifted her head and smiled at his mother. "Oh yes. I'm interested. Do you have embarrassing photos of him too?"

Lu-Lu perked up and snapped her finger. "Oh yea, I got those too. I have pictures of him when he knocked a big bruise on his head. He tried to hit a rubber ball with a baseball bat. It took a nasty bounce. I know where that picture is."

"Mom!" Jack shouted. "Can we do that next time?"

"Oh no, honey, I'll be back." Lu-Lu stood up and left the table.

Jack sat back in his chair. He was in a no-win situation with his mom. Katie reached under the table and held his hand.

She whispered to him, "Don't be embarrassed. I wish I had my mom to show embarrassing pictures of me."

Jack's tense face relaxed.

"Fun family, huh." Tyler said. "I love my wife. She's a hoot."

"Here it is." Lu-Lu brought a picture of eight-year old Jack with a patch on the left side of his forehead. She looked at his face and now noticed the remnants of the bruise from years ago.

"Are you done embarrassing me?" He asked and smiled at his mother.

"Almost." She winked. "Did your mom tease you and show your baby pictures?"

Katie replied. "She passed away when I was twelve so I don't have a lot of pictures of her. My parents had a lot of pictures of me but not themselves."

"I'm sorry for your loss. That's what happens with parents. We get these kids and go gaga over them. Do you have kids?"

Katie coughed. "No, I don't."

"Have you been married before?" Lu-Lu asked and grabbed the barbecue sauce from the middle of the table.

Jack interrupted her mid-chew with roast pork in his teeth. "Mom. Slow down. This isn't the inquisition."

Katie forked the green beans casserole and answered "It's okay. Yes, I have. Twice. No kids from either one." She took a bite and savored the flavor. "This is really tasty."

"Thank you, sweetie. Family recipe." Lu-Lu beamed with pride. "How long have you been seeing each other?

She jerked. "We're not—"

"About a month." Jack took his napkin and wiped the barbecue sauce from his face. "We met at Lisa's wedding."

"That's so sweet." Lu-Lu said and smiled at Katie and Jack. "Isn't Lisa expecting her first child?"

"We could use more grandkids." Tyler and Lu-Lu both looked at Katie, who choked on her sweet tea.

Jack patted her back. "Are you okay?"

"Yes." She said while still trying to control her cough.

"Too soon?" Tyler asked and poured more barbecue sauce over his pulled pork. He broke pieces of cornbread on top of it.

"Dad! You're as bad as mom. What's going on? You're both usually better behaved than you are now." He looked over at Katie and apologized. "Sorry, my family speaks their mind and there's no holding back."

Katie laughed and coughed so hard that tears flowed into her eyes and rolled down her cheeks. She dabbed the tears with her napkin.

"It's getting late and I promised her ice cream." Jack rose from the table and cleared the dishes.

"I'll help." Katie said. She collected the glasses and followed him to the kitchen.

"Put them in the dishwasher." Lu-Lu called out from the table.

Jack loaded the plates in the dishwasher as his mother requested. He scrubbed a few of the big pots and pans. Katie found a black checkered dishtowel to dry them.

"Sorry about the romantic dinner. I wanted you to meet my parents. I don't know what's wrong with them. They're outspoken but not normally this outrageous."

"They want you to live your life." She said. "My father is about control. Your parents are about having fun. How much fun have you had since Paige passed away?"

"Not much. I bury myself in yardwork. The satisfaction of creating a paradise filled with exotic plants, shrubs and grasses gives me something to accomplish."

Katie thought about what he said. They were very similar in dedicating their lives to their work.

"All clean?" Lu-Lu asked when she entered the kitchen. Tyler was outside and ignited the wood in the fire pit. "Are you staying? We can roast marshmallows."

"I've got to get her back home before it's too late," he answered.

"Oh," Lu-Lu smiled and nodded. "Go make me some grandbabies. I'm gonna quit teasing after this."

Lu-Lu hugged Katie and whispered in her ear. "Paige said he was good in bed. Go find out for yourself."

Katie's cheeks turned bright red after Lu-Lu's suggestion.

Jack looked at the pair with curiosity and wonderment.

"What did you say, Mom?" He leaned over and hugged her.

"Oh nothing, honey. Just girl talk. You take her out for ice cream. Waffle House has a good breakfast if you two don't feel like cooking in the morning."

Jack kissed his mom on the cheek. "Bye, Mom. Tell Dad we're leaving."

"Okay honey. Tyler!" his mother left to find his father.

"Let's get out of here before she brings out more pictures." Jack smiled and shook his head. "Bless her heart. I love my Mom."

***

"Brewster's for ice cream?" He asked.

"I can't have the calories. My clothes are getting tight." She moaned.

What is it with this family? I'm always eating.

"Okay, I'll take you home."

"Thank you for dinner and the train ride. I can say that I've had the second best Southern cuisine in town."

"Second best?" The lines creased in his forehead and he tightened his grip on the steering wheel."

"Yes." She smiled. "May makes the best Southern cuisine."

Katie looked over at him and could see the pride in his eyes.

"She wants to go to chef school."

"That's great." She yawned. "Why did you tell your parents that we're seeing each other?"

He shrugged. "It seemed like a good idea at the time."

She had such a good time today that she didn't care to debate the status of their relationship.

She shook her head and yawned again.

"Oh, I'm sorry. It's not the company. I've been so tired lately and I don't know why. I'm normally up later than this working on projects but I'm going to bed as soon as you drop me off."

"Fair enough."

Katie rummaged her purse to look for her phone. She pulled it out to turn it on.

Dead.

No calls from the office and if there were any, she'd missed them.

"Is everything okay at the office?" He asked.

"I wouldn't know. The phone is dead." She said disappointed with the status of her electronic lifeline.

"It may be a good thing. You can get some rest tonight without any disturbance."

Katie closed her eyes and reclined the seat back. The next time she opened her eyes she was in her driveway.

"We're here."

He parked the SUV and got out of the car. He stood on the passenger side, opened the door and reached for her hand. She stood up. He closed the door and she looked up at him.

"Did you have a good nap?" He asked.

"Uh, yes, I'm sorry. It's been a long day." She said and reached into her purse for the house keys.

"I think I'd better leave." He said.

"Thank you. I had fun with you this evening."

He took her in his arms and pressed his lips against her forehead. He then brushed his lips against her ear and softly spoke to her. "Goodnight."

"Goodnight."

CHAPTER 19

"Oh, why does that damn alarm go off so early?" moaned Katie. She peeked through her eyelids and looked at the alarm clock. It was time to get up.

"I don't understand," she yawned and crawled out of bed. "I went to bed as soon as I got home from helping April and May redecorate their rooms and I still haven't finished all of my work."

This morning was going to be a busy one. Katie got up and searched the closet for her favorite blue dress to wear for a customer visit.

"Well this is a little snug for a company lunch. Let me pull out the navy blue. It's the largest dress in my closet. I'll schedule more time with Mario. I don't understand why my clothes are too tight."

May.

I've got to stop eating at the Williams household three to four times a week. These past couples of months have ruined my diet.

I would never hurt May's feelings by turning down dessert.

She smiled at her reflection in the mirror. Her midsection had a slight bulge. She brushed her hand over it and smoothed out any wrinkles in her dress. Suddenly an urge to go.

Damn.

I'm going to be late.

Into the bathroom she went. Five minutes later, she finished dressing and rushed down the stairs to get in her car and fight Atlanta traffic. Turning on her favorite pop radio station, she sang along to the tunes. Her cell phone rang and interrupted her private concert.

"Oh, not now. I bet it's the office."

She was at a traffic light when she answered.

"Yes, Katrina."

"Mr. Woo is here. He's in the Rhenus Room."

"Thank you. Tell him I'll be there soon. There's a traffic jam on I-285 and it will take me a little bit longer to get there."

"Will do."

She hung up, blinked her eyes and reflected on how strange her health had been over the past few weeks. Trips to the bathroom were frequent as well as a few times in the middle of the night. She suffered from pure exhaustion and required more rest than usual. She would consult her doctor for B12 shots and hope that it would resolve the matter.

"I've got too much work to do. I can't be this tired all the time."

***

"Yes, Katrina, Mr. Woo was impressed with my knowledge. I'm meeting him for dinner in a few. Make sure to make extra copies for the presentation tomorrow. I have to go. I'm almost here."

Katie was a few minutes away from Dupree Country Club when she wrapped up her conversation at the office. She arrived minutes later and parked not far away from the entrance to the bar.

Her customer hadn't arrived yet so she went in. She noticed Doug Bader alone seated at the bar and approached him.

"Hi, Doug."

He settled his vodka martini on the bar napkin and stood up to greet her with a shallow hug. "It's good to see you. How's the new soccer mom?"

She laughed. "I'm just friends with the family. I didn't realize that soccer took up so much time. I don't know how those families do it or afford it. How's married life, Doug? Is it what you expected?"

He offered her the empty bar stool next to him.

She shook her head and declined. "I'm waiting for clients."

He shrugged his shoulders, nodded his head and continued to answer her question. "Actually, pretty good. We're taking one of the rooms and making it into a nursery. Lisa didn't want to know what we're having so it's going to be a surprise. It's hard to plan a nursery if you don't know what you're having."

Katie wasn't jealous. Her feelings for him diminished over time. Her needs were fulfilled. Jack and the girls gave her a new perspective on what's important.

"That's great." She called out to the bartender. "Cosmo please."

Doug looked at her and the bartender both. He held up the palm of his hand in order to stop the conversation from continuing. He said sternly, "I wouldn't drink that if I were you."

"Why?" She couldn't believe Doug was interfering with her personal freedom to have a drink. She was off work and was entitled to relax prior to meeting a client. One drink wouldn't hurt her.

"You're pregnant."

"What?" She exclaimed.

That's absurd!

Has he lost his mind?

"You're pregnant. Is this good news or bad news for you? I felt sure that you were pregnant last week when I saw you at the soccer tournament."

"That's impossible. Two husbands ran off with other women because I couldn't get pregnant. How would you know if I'm pregnant?"

"I've been nicknamed the human pregnancy test. I can guess it within a few days of conception. My recent victims were my secretary, Rebecca, Harold's wife, Hannah, and of course my lovely wife, Lisa."

"Didn't you hear me? I just told you I can't get pregnant."

"Humor me. Please don't drink that until you have a pregnancy test." She looked at Doug's stoic face and felt the gravity of his message. "I'll order something else for you." Doug waved his hand to get the attention of the bartender. "Perrier for the lady."

"Hmm. Good choice." She nodded in agreement. She picked up her wrist and looked at her watch. "Mr. Woo should be here any minute."

***

Early Saturday morning, Katie went to the studio for Pilates stretches. Mario was available for the extra session she requested. She put on a leotard and noticed that the bulge from yesterday seemed a little more noticeable and a lot firmer.

I hope today's session will work this off.

"Are you ready for today's stretches?" The sound of Mario's sweet southern twang interrupted her thoughts. Now she must get serious and focus on trimming her tummy.

"Yes."

The lesson was completed a half hour later.

"Stand up straight honey. You seem off balance." Katie pulled in her abdomen and stiffened her shoulders.

"Do you mind?" Mario placed his hand on her stomach.

"Umph, Umph, Umph." He placed his finger to his lips and a hand on his hip. He walked around her to continue his assessment.

"What's wrong?"

"Have you been to the doctor lately?" Mario's eyes crinkled with concern.

"No. Why?" She was worried by the high pitch tone in Mario's voice. Although he was gay, this was higher than normal.

"You are p-r-e-g-n-a-n-t pregnant."

Not again.

What is it with these men?

I'm not cut out to be a mother.

I don't have time for that!

She scowled. "You are the second man to tell me that I'm pregnant. I told him and I will tell you, I can't have children. Two husbands left me because of it."

He waved his hand and dismissed her concerns. "Maybe those two husbands didn't have what it takes. Whoever you are messing with now has knocked you up, girlfriend."

Katie stared back at him.

How can that be? She hadn't been with anyone since Doug and that was a long time ago.

Uh oh, wait a minute. Valentine's Day.

No way!

"I'll get a pregnancy test today and shut you and Doug Bader up. This is absurd. I can't be pregnant."

***

Katie sat in her car after Pilate's class still thinking about what Mario and Doug told her.

Those men don't know what they're talking about.

How would a man know anything about a woman being pregnant?

Women have to take a pregnancy test to find out for sure.

"That's it! I'll get a home pregnancy test. Why waste my time at the doctor? I can't be pregnant."

She drove to the grocery store that was closest to her home. She walked down the aisle labeled feminine products and saw several brands of pregnancy tests.

I can't believe I'm standing here buying a pregnancy test.

This is a waste of time.

I am NOT pregnant!

She reached and grabbed a box off the shelf. "This one will do."

The express line was long at the grocery store. She only had one item and it made sense to her to go to a regular line. The woman in front of her had a small child and several groceries. She appeared to be short of money and the cashier began to remove items from the cart.

The anxiety of taking the test was high. The conversation between the woman and the cashier was testing her patience.

"How much does she owe?" Katie demanded.

"Ma'am, I can handle my business." The woman responded.

Katie pulled a fifty-dollar bill out of her purse and handed it to the cashier. "Give her the damn groceries and this should cover the rest."

The cashier and the woman were both startled by Katie's outburst. The cashier accepted the money and the woman lightly protested.

"But ma'am. I can put stuff back."

"Not today. I need to get out of here and you're holding me up."

"I have change." The cashier said. "Who do I give it to?"

"Give it to her. She needs it." Katie demanded and slung her purse over her shoulders.

"Thank you, ma'am." The woman said and gathered her groceries. Her little boy smiled at Katie before they walked away.

"That was nice." The cashier said to Katie while ringing up the purchase. "Not many people do random acts of kindness."

Katie shook her head. "I had it. She needed it and I hope to God I'm not pregnant."

***

She arrived at her house shortly after leaving the grocery store. Taking the box to the bathroom, she read the instructions.

"This seems simple enough,"

The kit had two tests. She pulled out the first one and waited for the results. The indicator turned pink!

"This can't be right."

She stared at the test in disbelief and pulled the other test out of the box. A few minutes later, the second test turned pink as well.

"I can't believe it!" she hysterically screamed.

"I *am* pregnant!"

***

Katie made an urgent doctor's appointment.

She took a third pregnancy test.

Doug and Mario both were both right.

She felt sick.

She returned to the examination room and sat in bewilderment. The doctor came in later and confirmed the pregnancy test. The doctor talked about the results and all she heard was a faint voice in the distance. The only thing that echoed in her head was that she was in the early stages of becoming a mother.

She walked out of the office completely mystified by the news. Two failed marriages produced no children but a one-night stand did? How did he do that?

"This can't be happening to me."

She sat in her car and started the engine.

"What am I doing having a baby with a man who works in the yard? I date doctors, attorneys and multimillionaires. I'm a Pennington. Money and appearance are important to me."

A flash of the future went through Katie's mind. She saw herself stuck in the house with eight children, no money and Jack running off with another woman.

There's no way I'm telling him.

I'm not doing that again. I caught enough husbands in bed with other women.

I have to leave.

Leave.

That's it. I'm leaving town.

She'd call Arthur to see if she could transfer her job temporarily to Savannah. She was looking for an employee to work at that location. She could move there, interview the replacement and return to Atlanta after the baby was born.

She pulled into her driveway and passed by her new mailbox. She entered her house through the garage and plopped on the couch.

Who do I call first?

"Joey!"

She punched the keypad on the phone as fast as she could. He answered after the third ring.

"Joey speaking"

"Joey, are you in town? I have to talk to you." She paced the floor to channel her pent-up energy.

"Yes, do you want me to come by? Are you okay?"

"Yes, Joey, please and hurry."

He arrived thirty-five minutes later. She heard the doorbell ring and after opening the door, Joey was standing there with a worried look on his face.

"It sounded pretty important so I dropped everything and came over. Are you sure you're okay?"

She said frantically, "Come in. No, I'm pregnant."

He looked at her in disbelief as he was walked past her to come inside. "What? Are you okay with that?"

"I don't know. I haven't completely digested this yet. I need a really big favor from you."

"Anything. Just name it."

"Do you still have your house in Savannah?"

"Yes."

"I'm asking for a temporary transfer. I want to have the baby there. Can I live in your house temporarily?"

"Yes, I will set that up but why can't you tell him?" He asked.

"Because I need to work this out on my own." Katie said. "Trust me on this please."

CHAPTER 20

"All set for Savannah. Your new office is ready. They're expecting you in three weeks."

Katie still had her head down reviewing the export log and barely heard Katrina's news. She was leaving for Savannah and her workload was increasing. She had difficulty finding a worthy export manager and now that she's leaving, she'll be required to hire a replacement for Andy soon.

"Thank you. I have to make a few calls. We'll talk in about thirty minutes."

She picked up the stack of resumes and skimmed through the names and credentials. Twelve resumes and none of them met her criteria. Andy's replacement will be very hard to find and she doesn't have time to work with a recruiter.

She looked at her inbox in the left-hand corner of her desk and glanced at the cream-colored paper mixed in the stack of work that she didn't have time to do. She pulled the paper out of the box and glanced at the yellow sticky note in the center of the resume. It was a resume forwarded to her from her co-worker, Greg Speaks.

"Maya Dunbar."

She read the details of Maya's resume. Although she didn't specifically have a lot of experience with export, her contracts and aerospace background was impressive.

Katie remembered her casual conversation with Greg regarding her growing duties. He recommended Maya and forwarded her resume to Katie.

"Thank you, Greg. She may be the answer to my dilemma."

She dialed Maya's work number.

"Contracts, this is Maya."

"Hello, Maya. This is Katie Pennington. I work with Greg Speaks. Is this a good time to talk?"

"I can listen." She answered.

Katie swiveled in her chair and twirled the phone cord between her fingers. "Can you come in for an interview tomorrow afternoon at three-thirty?"

"Yes, I'll be there. Please give me the details."

Katie stopped swiveling and picked up her pen clicking it before writing the appointment in her calendar.

"Thank you for taking my call. I'll see you tomorrow."

***

Maya arrived for her interview on time dressed in a navy-blue suit with a white blouse. She was a light brown female with short-cropped curly hair. Although Katie didn't have any expectations on Maya's ethnicity but she was surprised by her plus sized weight.

"Welcome to Parker, Maya. Please, take a seat." Katie closed the door and the interview was underway.

"Thank you." She answered and set her maroon purse on the floor next to the chair. She placed her black portfolio on her lap.

Katie returned to her desk, picked up Maya's resume, and skimmed over it again. "I've been reviewing your resume and your name sounds familiar. Have we met before?"

Maya's eyebrows lifted in surprise. "No, I don't believe we have."

"How do you know Greg?" She asked.

Maya forced a smile. "He was the best man at my cousin, Lisa's, wedding."

Katie snapped her finger and pointed upward. "Yes, that's it. Coach Lisa!"

Maya smiled. "Yes, she's my first cousin. I was one of the bridesmaids at the wedding."

Katie exhaled softly. "I was there too. How are the newlyweds?"

Maya's stiffened shoulders now relaxed. She placed her hands in her lap. "They're doing wonderful. Are you a friend of Lisa's?"

"No, Doug." Katie abruptly switched the discussion to the job interview. She intertwined her fingers into a fist on her desk. "You come highly recommended by Greg Speaks. He is on track for Director of Marketing."

Maya nodded and smiled.

Katie unfolded her hands, picked up Maya's resume, and glanced over it. She lifted her forehead so she could make direct eye contact. "I thought that I'd speak to you immediately. I'll be working in the Savannah office. I need someone on staff here. Once my temporary transfer is over, I'll be back in town, but the position is permanent and full time."

"I've been looking for a change for a while and this sounds like a wonderful opportunity."

"Great. How soon could you get started? I need to leave right away."

"I'll have to give notice to my current employer. I can start two weeks after that."

"Good to know. I do have two other applicants coming in for interviews in the next few days as well, but I'd let you know as soon as a decision has been made."

***

Katie arrived in the driveway of her father's Dunwoody home. She parked in front of his three-car garage and used her remote to come in through the kitchen. He was waiting for her in the breakfast room that overlooked the outdoor the pool.

"I'm glad you made the time to come see your dad." He rose from his seat and hugged his daughter lightly.

She took a seat beside him at the kitchen table.

It was an unusually hot day for the month of April and she was exhausted from the drive, which only took fifteen minutes from the office. She plopped in her seat and tried to compose herself. This was going to be a difficult conversation.

"Do you want to sit by the pool?" He asked.

She felt dehydrated and wanted to quench her thirst. She grabbed the glass in front of her and poured sweet tea in it from the pitcher on the table.

"Are you getting enough rest?"

She sighed. "I'll be fine, Dad. I really need to talk to you." She drew a deep breath. She may as well get this conversation done and over with.

He offered her more sweet tea and she waived it away.

"I'm taking a temporary transfer to Savannah."

He smiled at the news. "A promotion? Good job, Tiger." His face beamed with pride.

"No, I just want to leave town." She reached across the table to pour the sweet tea she'd just declined a moment ago. She wished she could have a stronger drink but tea would have to do for the next several months.

"Why?" He questioned and leaned forward in his chair. "Those two jokers you married are gone. Did something happen at the office?"

"I'm pregnant, Dad."

He rose from his chair. "You're what!? When did this happen?"

She sighed and put her head in her hands. "Sit down."

"Are you sure? What happened?"

"I can't talk to you if you're going to stand over me. Please sit down."

He sat in a chair across from her.

She lifted her head and looked at the concern in her father's eyes. She knew this was news her father wasn't expecting and this announcement was stunning.

He sighed. "That's no reason to leave town."

"I've made up my mind. I'm staying at Joey's place in Savannah." Her racing heart slowed down after sharing the news. She let out a sigh of relief and picked up the tea to take in more fluids. She still felt flushed and didn't want to be hospitalized for not taking care of herself.

"I'm going to be a grandfather?" Her father's eyes widened as he digested the news.

She was so absorbed in her own life that she hadn't thought of ever being a mother let alone her father becoming a grandfather. More questions were coming and she was exhausted.

"Yes, you are." She confirmed.

Although relieved to break the news, she had a lot to do to prepare for the baby's arrival. Savannah would be a great place to escape temporarily. What was she going to do with a baby when she got back?

"I'm here to help you. Did you tell the baby's father?"

"No, and that's why I'm leaving town."

"Is it Joey's?"

"No, it's not," She said emphatically. "I've been telling you for years that we're just friends. Why can't you accept that?"

He shrugged. "Is the father married?"

She shook her head from side to side and shouted. "I don't mess with married men."

Now was not the time for judgement. She wasn't ready to reveal her sex life to her father and hadn't totally forgiven him for the Melinda thing. "I just don't want him to know. This is my problem and I'm handling it."

"It's also his responsibility to pay for the baby. Let me know who he is and I'll take care of it." Don lowered his jaw and looked Katie in the eyes.

"No. I don't know what I want to do. I need time to think."

"Termination? I can pay for that too if you—"

"Dad! I would never! You know how hard it's been for me to get pregnant in the past!" She stood up at the complete absurdity of her father's assumption.

He stood up as well and insisted that she sit back down. "I'm sorry, Tiger. I want to help. Don't rush off. You don't look like you feel well and you could use some rest."

She fought back a wave of tears she didn't understand and didn't want to acknowledge. "Thanks, Dad. I'm going to take a nap in my room. I know I have a lot to do but I can't do it all. I need rest."

"I don't want you lifting anything for the move. This is my grandchild. I'll arrange to have everything done for you. I don't want you to hurt yourself or the baby."

"Thank you."

She smiled and hugged him, letting the emotions go, not having to worry for one minute, maybe.

Too many decisions.

CHAPTER 21

She'd avoided telling Jack and his family goodbye long enough. It had been nearly a month and a half since she'd last seen them, always putting off plans, canceling at the last minute like she hated to do, but she just couldn't...

Katie took a breath.

She arrived at April's last soccer game of the season. She sat in the car for fifteen minutes wrapping up the last-minute details of her move. Her bags were packed for the long drive that was coming after this visit.

She waited for the whistle to blow at the end of the game so she could talk to the family as they were leaving the field. She slowly got out of the car and approached Jack's SUV. This time, she wore designer sneakers, pressed dark slacks and a loose sea green silk shirt. She hoped her swelling belly wouldn't be noticeable.

No one on the soccer team knew about her condition and she wanted to keep it that way. She stood next to his SUV and looked across the field. She saw Jack and the girls on their way.

The girls ran up to her.

"Hi Katie, we won. I wish you could've seen the game."

"It was a good one." Jack said.

"I like your sneakers." May said.

This was going to be more difficult than she thought.

Katie forced as confident a smile to her lips as she could manage, drew in a deep breath. "I came to tell you goodbye. I've been transferred to Savannah to start a new job."

It took a minute for the information to sink in.

And while it was the girls she spoke to, she couldn't help but look up into Jack's gaze, watch as the knowledge settled over him, the smile he'd worn to greet her thinning before disappearing in disbelief.

"But you can't!"

"You don't have to come to anymore of my games, Katie! I won't ask anymore! You don't have to drive me or anything, just don't leave!"

Oh God.

She'd known it was going to be hard.

She'd known that telling the girls was going to be bad, and she'd known they would plead and beg and cry, that she'd cry too.

But she'd expected Jack to say something.

Anything.

He just stared at her, shook his head. "Come on, girls, Miss Katie said she has to go. Her job's important to her and this is probably a big career move for her."

She heard the underlying sentiment to his words.

Her job's more important than us.

The girls didn't seem to notice, their arms around her waist growing tighter.

Her breathing, already strained from the rising pregnancy, grew fainter, or maybe that was panic and fear and sorrow at leaving.

"Will you come visit us at least?

"Can we come visit you?" April asked.

"Yes, of course, I'd love that." Katie wiped the tears from her cheeks with the back of her hand. "We'll arrange time for that."

"But why?" May cried.

"I have to." Katie hugged the sobbing girl.

"Who's going to take me to practice? All the other girls have their moms with them." April wailed.

Moms?

Does she consider me her mom?

"But we'll miss you!" May cried.

"I'll miss you too." This was too much for Katie to deal with.

The leaving. The pregnancy.

His silent stare, condemning and unbelieving at once.

Jack's lips were pressed firmly together and his dark eyes were cold and solid like marbles. He drew a deep breath and exhaled a few words. "Good luck on your new position."

He reached forward and put his hands on his daughter's shoulders, pulled them awkwardly away from her, held them back, a barrier between them.

She cleared her throat, matched his formality. "It's been a pleasure spending time with you and your family."

"It's been a pleasure having you with us."

April looked between the two of them.

Katie bit her lip at the hurt on the girl's face.

Jack pulled the keys from his pocket and handed them to his teenager. "Get in the car, girls, I'll walk Miss Katie to her car."

He extended his hand, waiting for her to take it, not letting her go after all.

"Thank you." She slowly placed her hand in his.

The five-minute walk to her car seemed like an eternity.

With a few quick steps, she leaned against the driver's side door. He closed the distance between them.

"Do you really have to take this position?"

"Yes, it's important to me."

His dark brown eyes gazed into hers giving her the I'm-available-for-your-pleasure expression. "You're important to me."

His sincere words passed through his lips and echoed in her heart. If she could clear a week off her calendar and book a trip for two on a private island somewhere with him...

No. Stick to the plan.

"That's kind of you but my career fulfills me."

"Don't use your dependence on your career to keep you from getting close to anyone. I really care about you. Stay," he brushed his hand against her cheek, "Stay here, with us. With me."

"Jack, that's sweet, but I—" Tears rolled down her cheeks. With a shake of her head, she pulled his face to hers, his lip to hers.

It was time for her to go. She pulled away and looked into his deep brown eyes.

"Are you sure this is what you want?" He asked.

"Yes." She breathed. More tears that wouldn't stop. She was a Pennington. Tears were reserved for the bathroom and in a private setting.

It's the pregnancy.

I can't tell him.

"I must go now. I don't want to get there too late in the evening. I have a lot to do."

He moved in to kiss her again and she placed her hand in the middle of his chest to stop him.

"We have to stop and I have to go."

He nodded and stepped back. She reached for the keys, opened the car and sat behind the steering wheel. She turned her head and looked out the window.

He was still standing there.

I can't stay.

She started the ignition and pulled out of the parking space with his kiss still on her mind.

CHAPTER 22

Katie had been gone for three weeks.

He felt it in the pit of his stomach.

Damn he missed her.

Jack watched a few minutes of the second day of ODP tryouts and walked to an empty bench away from the parents. He didn't want to socialize and would rather spend more time in the yard planting flowers and shrubs.

The stress of Katie's departure affected his entire household. April wasn't focusing in school and May wasn't sleeping at night, always wanting to climb into bed with him. He kept pushing her to sleep with April instead.

He couldn't let on to the girls that he missed her the most.

His phone rang.

He reached in his pocket and pulled it out.

He sighed when he recognized the number.

"Hello, Mom."

"How's my son?" She asked.

"I'm fine."

"Have you heard from Katie yet?"

"No, ma'am." He stood from the bench and stretched his free arm towards the sky.

"When are you going to bring her home? You need her."

"She's gone, Momma."

"Until you bring her back. Listen. You've only brought home two women to meet me and you married both of them. This one is special to you. Find her and bring her back."

Katie *was* special to him.

He'd always had a thing for strong independent women and Katie fit the bill to a "T."

He adored her.

No, if he was honest, it was more than adoration he felt for her. For the way she took care of his girls. The way she seemed to gravitate to him even though they both knew she didn't need to. She was her own person, but needed someone in her life as much as he needed someone in his.

And Jack couldn't understand why she'd left him.

"She's gone, Mom. Nothing to it. April's in the middle of tryouts right now. I have to go."

"Don't lose out on love, Son, just because you're afraid of going for what you want. I love you. Take care of my grandbabies."

"I love you too, Mom. Bye."

Looking across the field at April, he remembered how excited she'd been to introduce him to Katie.

When they danced at the wedding, he hadn't wanted to let her go.

The mere fact that she released her calendar to open her time and heart to his family, allowed him to see her personality beyond the corporate executive.

How could he find Katie and convince her to come back to Atlanta?

Where would he start?

Coach Lisa.

Maybe she could talk to Doug.

Katie said that they were friends.

It was easy enough to dial the number he'd memorized so long ago to speak to his daughter's coach.

"Lisa speaking."

He felt awkward disturbing her in the middle of a Saturday afternoon, but his daughters had needs that he couldn't fill.

And he had needs that maybe he shouldn't be ignoring either.

"Afternoon, Coach Lisa, this is Jack speaking, April Williams' dad from your soccer team. Do you have a minute?"

"Sure. Is this about the ODP tryouts? How's April doing?"

"No, no, nothing about that. She's doing well."

"Oh good. Well what can I do for you, Jack?"

A train horn sounded in the background of the call.

"It sounds like you're out. I can call another time."

"I'm stuck behind a slow-moving train. I'm not going anywhere, so what's up?"

"I don't know if you remember Katie Pennington."

"Yes, she's a friend of my husband. She brought April to practice a few times and came to the games. I haven't seen her lately."

"That's because she took a job transfer to Savannah. I haven't heard from her since she moved. The girls and I really miss her. I promised them that I would do what I could to find her and bring her back. Is there anything that you or Doug can do to help us?"

"I'll talk to Doug. You'll hear from us soon."

"Thanks, Coach. Bye."

"Bye."

***

Jack received a call from Lisa to meet her at the Dupree Country Club. She was in the lobby waiting for him when he walked in. She led him to the bar where Doug was sitting with an older, grey-haired gentleman.

Doug kissed Lisa on the cheek before nodding to Jack and turning to the gentleman at his side to make the introductions. "Don, you remember my wife Lisa? And this is Jack Williams, he's the father one of the girls on Lisa's soccer team."

Jack extended his hand to Don and wondered why he was here being introduced to this gentleman.

"Don Pennington."

Katie's father.

The firm handshake suggested a strong business background, a tycoon, just like the daughter who'd disappeared.

Jack forced himself not to noticeably stand taller, pretend he was at ease in this meeting of this wealthy white-collar individual who held his future in his hands.

"Thanks for the introduction, Doug."

"Hope everything works out, Jack." Doug and Lisa walked away from the pair.

"I appreciate you taking the time to talk to me."

Don nodded and motioned for Jack to take the seat next to him at the bar. "What can I do for you, son?"

Jack cleared his throat. "I have to find your daughter, Sir."

Don leaned back in his chair. His black and grey eyebrows creased towards the center of his nose. His eyes bored into Jack's "Why?"

"She developed a good friendship with my girls and I miss her very much."

Don's frown relaxed into a smile. "April and May?"

"You know about them?" Jack's dark brown eyes perked up. He was unaware that Katie had mentioned his family to anyone.

She rarely talked about anyone or anything outside of work.

"Yes, I do. She calls and talks about them all the time. She misses them too. Are you their father?"

"Yes, Sir, I am. I love my girls and would do anything for them. I really have to find Katie. I mean, for my daughters, of course." Jack hoped he was successful persuading Don to help him find her.

"The next time I talk to her I'll let her know to call them." Don motioned to the bartender to come over.

"Wait," Jack grabbed Don's shoulder, the desperate hold making the old man stiffen in his grip. "Sir, please."

Don turned back to Jack.

"Mr. Pennington, I'm in love with your daughter. I need to find her." To settle his quivering stomach, he drew in a deep breath and exhaled. "I need to bring her home."

Don stared at him, considered, then nodded for the bartender.

Jack's heart sank.

Don casually reached into his suit jacket, pulled out a business card and handed it to Jack. "This is against my better judgement."

Jack reached across the bar and accepted the card.

"Call this number and talk to my secretary. I have a private plane that will leave for Savannah at 10:00 a.m. tomorrow. Be there. Arrangements will be made to take you to her residence." Don's drink arrived and he leisurely took a sip.

Jack stood up and extended his hand. "Thank you."

Don stood up gripped his hand. "Good luck."

CHAPTER 23

He had to make plans at least for an overnight stay.

The girls were at day camp so he'd need someone to watch them in the evening. His mother wouldn't mind, she always loved taking care of the grandbabies.

That was the easiest part of his plan.

The hardest part would be getting on the plane, not knowing what to say when he got off and came face to face with the woman he needed to see.

Jack sank back into his seat on the private jet and watched the runway disappear out the window as the pilot took off from the Cherokee County airport.

He loved her.

She'd stayed late a few nights to tuck the girls into bed, even read stories to May a time or two. No one else had ever taken an interest in April, not even April's biological mother, but Katie had.

She'd seen his family, and even when she hadn't wanted to be part of it, she was.

She'd helped him, not even knowing it.

She filled a space in his heart he hadn't thought would ever be filled again after Paige passed.

Hell, they'd only had sex that once, and, well, yeah, he wouldn't mind sleeping with the beautiful lady again, but he loved being around her more, loved sparring with her, loved making her laugh, or blush, or deny she wanted another helping of May's apple cobbler.

Somehow, despite the way his kids were, despite their need for a mother in their lives, it was him who Katie mattered to the most, because she filled all the roles he needed, those spots he'd thought were empty for good.

Katie was an important part of his family.

And he was going to get her to come home.

***

He arrived at a beachfront condominium on Tybee Island in coastal Savanna, Georgia. He stepped out of the limousine Don had sent for him and was blasted with extreme heat and gusty winds from the ocean.

Looking at the address in hand, he stepped to the door and knocked.

She opened the door.

"Katie."

Her mouth dropped opened and she raised a hand to her throat, stepped back but not like she was trying to get away, almost like his presence was so shocking that it was all she could do to take him in.

He dropped his overnight bag on the ground. "I thought you fell off the face of the earth."

He moved to hug her and she didn't resist him.

I'm never letting her go.

When he backed away, she looked up into his eyes and he pressed his lips against hers with light tenderness, let the kiss morph into something smoldering with need. He felt her tense body relax in his arms.

He pulled away and gazed into her eyes.

Her lips parted.

He waited for her to speak.

Silence.

Not Katie's style. She was a woman who knew how to take the commanding way.

Maybe it's my unexpected appearance.

Maybe it's hers.

She didn't have on any makeup standing in front of him. Her clothes weren't designer, he didn't think, just a loose yellow sundress and flat sandals, not the elegant executive he was used to her being. She'd put on some weight finally, looked good with the extra flush to her skin.

"How did you find me?" She asked.

"Your dad."

"My Dad? He wouldn't never have—"

He covered her mouth with his lips over hers before she could say another word. "I really missed you."

She shoved him away. "I don't miss you! I don't want you here!"

He stepped back, yielding the distance she demanded though he kept his hands on her wrists, would have twined his fingers with hers but she'd balled them into fists. "Are you going to be a good hostess and let me in?"

"No way! How did you find me? I need time to think. I need—" She gagged, turned away from him, and puked in the grass next to the sidewalk.

Jack stood behind her, pulled her hair away from her face. He looked at her driveway and noticed the only car parked in it was hers. "That must have been some party last night. I'll get something to settle your stomach for that hangover."

"The hell you will!" She wiped her mouth with her arm. "I can take care of myself."

"Not now you can't." He offered his arm for support. "You have to lie down. You could get dehydrated." He pushed the front door open and led her inside.

She plopped down on the couch and stretched her legs under the coffee table. Jack walked into the kitchen and brought back a cool towel. He leaned over and dabbed her forehead.

"This should help."

"Five more months of this shit," she mumbled.

"Five more months of what?" He asked.

"Not your concern. Why don't you go home?" She sneered.

"Because you need me." He grinned. He watched as she curled up on the couch. He grabbed the rose-colored blanket that was on the other end, covered her, and fluffed the pillows under her head.

She looked tired. Very tired.

"Why are you really here, Katie?" He asked.

"Maybe because I'm pregnant." She said angrily with a bit of sarcasm.

Pregnant?

April's homecoming dance…

No raincoats.

"Mine?" He asked.

"Maybe, maybe not. What does it matter? I don't want you here for this. You'll just leave. Everyone always does."

He frowned as he met her stare. "I'm not going anywhere."

"Fuck you, Jack." She snatched the blanket and covered part of her head with it. "It's definitely yours, dammit. Yours, asshole. One fucking time on Valentine's day."

"Why didn't you just tell me?"

Katie pushed herself off the couch, stood, and faced him. "Maybe because I didn't want you to feel sorry for me, to feel obligated to me."

What about her obligations to me? What about my girls?

She could learn to deal with it, doing something for someone else for once!

"We're going home."

"Home!" She snapped her head back and shouted. "I'm not leaving."

Well fuck that, you're already part of my family and I'm not leaving without you!

"And, we'll pick up a marriage license..."

"Marriage license! I'm not getting married again and certainly not to you." She stepped back and bumped her calf against the couch. She didn't realize there wasn't a lot of room to get away. He grabbed her arms to keep her from falling. He stepped back pulled her towards him and gave her some floor space from the couch.

"Oh yes you are. I'm not up for a nasty custody battle. My girls will get hurt in the process. Our baby, my name. That includes you too. We're going back tonight. We'll call your dad to make the arrangements."

"You literally asked me to marry you for the sake of our unborn baby and you don't want a custody battle. Fuck you!"

"Maybe that wasn't the way to ask…"

"It certainly wasn't the most memorable proposal of the century." She snarled back at him.

"We can argue about that on the plane back to Atlanta. Where's your suitcase? I'll pack it for you."

"No way! You're not packing my suitcase!" She drew back and crossed her arms, hugging herself to keep away from Jack. "I don't answer to you."

He shrugged and turned away, moved through the house like he owned it, guessing at where to go and she followed behind, fuming.

"Didn't you hear me? I'm not leaving with you." She grabbed his arm.

He turned to face her, his body moving to force her against the wall, cage her with his greater height and mass. He pressed his hands to the wall on either side of her, keeping her pinned without touching her.

Her chest rose and fell with frantic breaths.

"Didn't you hear me?" He demanded, "I want you as my wife. I love you and I miss you. I'm not leaving without you."

She crossed her arms across the top of her abdomen. "No!"

"You're pretty damn stubborn." He reached into his pocket, pulled out his cell phone, and pressed the digits on the keypad. He placed the phone on his ear and waited for an answer.

"Who are you calling?" She demanded.

He waived her away so he could talk.

"Pennington." The voice said through the phone.

"Hello? Don, this is Jack. I'm bringing your daughter home. When can we get a flight out?"

She hurried to get in front of him, place her hands on his chest and push him back. "No! I'm not going anywhere!

Her strength didn't even phase him and he turned away and continued to talk.

"Tomorrow," Jack said. "Thanks. That would be great. You want to speak to your daughter? Hold on. Here she is." He stopped and turned back to her, her mouth hanging open as he handed her the phone.

His eyebrows rose when she just stared at him and he waited patiently for her to accept the call.

With a growl, she took the cell and raised it to her ear, "Daddy, look, you don't...But, Dad! ... Yes, Sir. ... Yes. ... Yes, Dad. ... Bye."

"What'd he say?" Jack asked.

"None of your business."

His eyes narrowed. He stared at her and demanded a response. "Tell me, Katie. What did he say?"

Her eyes met his with a cold stare. "He said to call the cops and have them arrest you."

"No, he didn't. Want to try again?"

"He said to get on the damn plane and we'd talk in Atlanta."

Jack's tense body relaxed. "Perfect. Looks like I'll be here overnight and we'll fly home together tomorrow."

"I'm a big girl, Jack. I've been on my own for a long time. I take care of myself and my job and I'm not leaving!" She gritted her teeth and snorted.

His voice softened hoping to ease her concerns. "Maybe it's time for us to take care of each other."

"Just let it go." She relaxed and sighed. "It's not going to work."

He brushed his lips against her ear. "It will. Trust me. Let's not argue anymore."

CHAPTER 24

His lips settled over hers and rested his palms on her behind. She placed her hands on his shoulders and drew him closer.

She couldn't remember a time when any of the men in her life came to her rescue.

Her father's solution was always to work hard and throw money at problems to make them go away.

Her ex-husbands found comfort in other beds but never tried to make themselves available to fulfill her needs.

She felt as though she were in the middle of a fairy tale.

Jack was here in Savannah. Her knight in shining armor wanting to whisk his princess bride away to his castle, and believing that picking up a marriage license will give them the happily-ever-after.

God, I hope he's right.

She wrapped her arms around his back and leaned into him. The fire in her blood at his touch soft and coaxing, a warm smolder to keep the chill at bay in the winter, and keep her happily content to bask in his heat during the summer. She rested her head against his chest, pressed her ear to his heart, and listened to the steady beat.

But the reality of the moment reigned in.

"I don't understand why you couldn't tell me. I deserved to know. Did you think that I would never find out?"

"I don't know. I didn't think that far ahead," She said despondently. "I just needed time to think."

"April and May trust you. What about them? Didn't they deserve to know about their brother or sister?"

She moved to wipe the tears from her eyes and he stopped her, cupped her chin in his work-roughened fingers and turned her gaze up to his. "I want to marry you, Katie. You're part of my family."

"Getting married is not the answer. Marriage would be a disaster."

"Why? We get along well. You love my girls. I think you have feelings for me. Why shouldn't we get married?"

"I've tried the marriage thing twice. It's too soon. We don't really know each other."

"We have plenty of time to get to know each other. As husband—" He pressed his lips softly against hers. "—*and* wife."

Though charmed by his sincerity, his words didn't ease her concerns. "Why are you willing to get married again? Because I'm pregnant? That's a horrible reason to get married, Jack. Lots of people have kids outside of wedlock these days."

He intertwined his fingers and rested his palms behind her back, drawing her in close to him. "From the moment I asked you to dance with me and you so graciously accepted, I knew there was more between us. You have a desire to be treated and accepted as a well-educated, intelligent woman. I'm not afraid of powerful women. I raise them. I love them. Have you ever gotten into a fight with April?"

She laughed.

April was a tough young lady and Jack had his hands full with her.

He'd balked at Katie's schedule but never degraded the importance of her career.

She sighed, "Jack—"

"Think about it, Katie. That's all I'm asking. Give life to your planner. Hell, plan us in your planner. You and me. We need each other. We're both hard workers and if we're not careful, we'll miss what's important; spending time with each other. I've lost that woman and I'm not prepared to lose you too."

Tears streamed down Katie's face. He brushed his lips against her moist cheeks. She whimpered softly.

"I'll make some dinner. You look tired and should rest." He picked up her hand and kissed her swollen fingers, the baby's influence already showing itself in her body.

"Oh no," she sniffled and laughed through her tears, "We'll eat at Teeples. I'm craving seafood and they have the best seafood in town.

***

Jack and Katie returned home from dinner. She unlocked the front door and he stood behind her.

Before she entered the condo, she turned to face him. "I was really surprised to see you."

"It looks like we're both are full of surprises."

They crossed the threshold. She locked the door and turned to place her hand in her favorite spot in the middle of his chest.

She wanted him naked. She wanted to remember the wanting and the undressing and the touching and kissing this time.

She wanted him.

She'd missed him.

He slid out of his button down and she slid her hands under his tee and raised it off over his shoulders.

He unbuckled his belt and his pants fell to the floor.

She glided her hands all over his well-defined muscles. She stretched to press her lips to his, tasting the hint of the glass of wine he'd had at dinner on his tongue, the bergamot delight that was his own unique taste beneath it.

She moaned when he pulled back, slid his hands up her arms, and cupped her face in his palms. "Slow down. I'm here."

"So am I. I want to forget everything else right now. I just want to feel you and me. I want to feel what it's like between us..." Because whatever happened in the morning, she wanted tonight.

Her hand stroked over his cotton covered erection and he stiffened further at her touch. She hooked a finger in the waistband of his boxers and stepped backwards, pulled him down the hall to her bedroom, where she made a tease of removing her clothes, the tease lasting only long enough for him to reach her, slip her panties from her hips and let them drop to the floor.

He stepped in close, slid his lips over hers, kissed her chin, her neck, trailed delicate touches over her shoulder as he leaned in and reached behind her, unhooked her bra and let it fall to the floor.

She returned the favor as best she could, running her fingers under the elastic line of his boxers until she grazed the firm mounds of his buttock, slipped the fabric over his skin in as sensual a caress as he'd done for her.

They stood there, entirely exposed to each other.

Her breath came rapidly.

He calmed her with a touch, drew her in to his body so she was surrounded with his warmth.

He lifted her gently and laid her on the bed, worshipped her flesh with teasing licks and nips, her hips rising to demand long before he was ready to allow her surcease, not nearly long enough as she found herself crying out when his body pierced deep into hers and the world burst with thousands of lights around her.

She moaned.

He sat back, still planted deeply within her, drew her into his arms so that she was sitting on his lap, knees bent at his hips.

"I love you. I messed up earlier, I know, but, Katie, I love you." He brushed back the hair from her forehead. "I love you."

Her fingers clenched at his shoulders. Each thrust of his body into hers made with another utterance of the three words she hadn't realized she'd wanted to hear so badly, wanted to say so badly in turn.

"Come for me, baby."

Her head tipped back with her second orgasm and he buried his whiskered cheek against her breast when he followed her over into bliss.

He laid them down on the bed, her chest to his, her head pillowed on her shoulder.

"I love you too," she whispered.

***

She didn't sleep well.

Her thoughts rolled around in her head like hornets chasing a bear.

Marriage. A baby. Being a mother. Being a mother to a teenager. Another husband. A little girl.

And what about her job? What about her life? Her work?

The family he was offering her?

Jack shifted in his sleep and pulled her closer. He reached until he found her hand pressed over his heart and tangled their fingers together with a light squeeze.

His breath rustled her hair. His heartbeat steadied her.

She relaxed with his strong arms to hold and protect her.

CHAPTER 25

He rose early and arranged for the flight back to Atlanta. He searched through her refrigerator to see what he could prepare for breakfast. He wanted Katie to continue to rest because he knew that it would be a long day and they had a lot to discuss.

He'd woken a few times during the night because she tossed and turned in her sleep. He'd placed his hands on her abdomen and caressed it, hoping it would calm both mother and child

While sipping on a cup of coffee, he heard her footsteps before she entered the kitchen.

She wore his shirt, the buttons hastily done, barely covering her breasts and exposing her abdomen and lilac panties beneath the ensemble. She rubbed her eyes and yawned. "We need to talk about the future, Jack, seriously."

He motioned for her to have a seat at the table. He poured a glass of orange juice and set it in front of her.

She waved it away. "I'm not ready for that yet. If I drink that, I'll need lots of ice and water in it."

He grabbed her glass and took it to the kitchen counter. He diluted the juice and came back to the table. "I haven't changed my mind on anything I said last night."

He placed the watered-down juice in front of her.

She took a whiff of it and debated whether her stomach was going to be good this morning or throw a tantrum like normal. Best not. "We're not in love with each other. This won't work."

"I told you I loved you last night."

"Last night you said a lot of things with emotion and lust clouding your judgment. We both did. They don't mean anything."

"Those words mean everything. I haven't said them to anyone since Paige died."

"And you're still mourning her, Jack."

"Yeah."

She looked up at him, having expected him to deny it.

"Yeah, Katie, all right? I am still mourning her. I'll always be mourning her because I loved her and I miss her but she wouldn't want me to spend the rest of my life alone, not when I've found someone who I can help mend that hurt with."

"This will never work. Men are all the same. They take what they want and move on to the next woman in line without looking back."

"Like Doug Bader? I mean, that's who you wanted, right, Katie? Someone rich and sophisticated? Everything I'm not."

She couldn't believe his nerve. She'd never told him about that part of her past and he'd made a big assumption. Albeit a true one. "That was low, Jack. We ended that long ago before he met Lisa. Why did you bring that up?"

He knew he'd struck a nerve but wanted to get it out of the way. If they were going to have a life together, certain things about each of their past relationships should be discussed right away. He didn't need a woman that felt that he was less of a man because he wasn't rich.

"I brought it up because you want a wealthy man. Someone your dad will approve of, someone that has a certain stature. Well, you had two marriages based on money and where are they now?"

Had he just called her a snob? Or, worse, was he implying she wanted a trophy husband?

"I make no apologies for being accustomed to a certain standard of living that you'll never be able to provide for me or this baby."

"Have you ever really been happy? Are you telling me that you were happier in those fake marriages than spending time with me and my daughters?"

No.

No, she'd never been happier before.

So why did he bring that up?

"You can't tell me that all you want in life is work. I've seen you change over the past few months. You took less calls at the office. You spent more time with me and the girls and you didn't throw out the caterpillars."

She laughed.

It was good to laugh again.

He does make me happy.

CHAPTER 26

Jack packed Katie's clothes quickly since the limousine arrived early. It was parked in the driveway ready to take them to the Savannah airport.

When they got in the limousine, she settled in her seat, picked up the phone and made a few calls. She called the Savannah office first. Then Maya to let the woman know Katie was taking some personal time off and that she was flying back to Atlanta.

Katie was sure that marrying Jack would be a huge mistake and couldn't imagine what her life would be like married to him. She wasn't interested in living a middle-class life or being married to a middle-class man.

She loved April and May dearly and wouldn't do anything to hurt them. She barely knew Jack.

How would they get along?

The sex was good, but that wasn't all a relationship was about and certainly not the only grounds to begin a marriage!

***

Jack thought about his daughters and how happy they would be when he brought Katie "*home*" for good as their new mother. He'd realized that he pressured Katie to get married but hoped she'd say yes.

He might not know everything about her, but what he knew he loved. She could be strong and independent by taking command of her career and her life. She was a great listener and it was easy to have conversations with her.

She was selfless with her time. He knew that there were nights she planned to devote to work. Instead she read May a story or helped April with her homework. She managed to sneak in a few moments to get to know him better.

He wanted to share more days and nights with her, living, loving laughing and learning her mind body and soul. They had a future together and he couldn't image spending it without her.

***

The Pennington family limousine was waiting for them on the tarmac when they got in.

As Jack and Katie debarked the plane, May and April jumped out of the limo and ran across the runway to come to them.

Don, Tyler and Lu-Lu climbed out after the girls and waited next to the car for everyone to walk towards them.

"Mom! Dad!" Jack smiled, not having expected his mother, or his father, as it turned out, to be waiting for him to bring Katie home.

Tyler grinned and hugged his wife while everyone got situated.

"It's good to see ya," Lu-Lu hugged Katie.

"What are you doing here?" Jack asked. He hugged his father fiercely before turning to offer his hand to Don.

Lu-Lu answered, "I called Mr. Pennington after you gave me his number in case of emergency. We talked for a long time."

Don nodded in agreement.

Lu-Lu pressed her hand against Katie's swollen abdomen. "Are you pregnant? Am I getting me a new grandbaby?"

Katie's cheeks were flushed. "Yes, ma'am, you are. I'm four months along."

Lu-Lu gave Katie a tight hug, smiling at her son over the slight woman's shoulder.

Jack offered a wan smile in return, nothing settled though he hoped things were on the right track.

April overheard the conversation and smiled at her dad. "Am I getting a little brother or sister? I really want this one."

Jack smiled indulgently but his voice brooked no argument when he responded. "Katie and I have a lot to discuss. Let it go for now."

CHAPTER 27

April and May were spending time with their grandparents so Jack and Katie could have time alone to talk. Both were exhausted from the long day that started in Savannah. They arrived at Katie's home.

Jack pulled in her driveway. "Give me your keys. I'm going to check the house out for you. You've been away a long time."

He wants to secure my house! No one ever does that for me.

"I have an alarm. Everything should be fine."

"Alright. I'll grab the bags."

She remembered to bring her garage door opener and they went into the house through the garage. After removing the alarm he followed her to the kitchen.

"I'll take these upstairs."

She looked around her palace which now seemed cold and empty. Everything was in place but something changed.

Maybe it was her.

He came back down the stairs and asked. "Have you got light bulbs? One's out in your bathroom in the master bedroom."

She'd knew the light was out before she'd left. She'd forgotten about it.

"They're in the linen closet."

"I'll go take care of it for you. I'll be right back." She watched him leave from the foyer.

Still assessing her house, she walked in her office. She spotted a leaflet from their time at Stone Mountain on her desk. She picked it up and stared at the pictures, could feel his arms around her as they'd been that day, his warmth.

Jack approached her office door. "By the way, I came by and fixed your porch swing while you were gone."

"You did?" She smiled at him and realized how short sided she'd been.

Their relationship wasn't about money or sex.

It was about taking care of each other.

It was about love.

I love him!

"Thank you." She breathed her words softly, placed her hand over her stomach and felt the baby flutter.

"Now that the house is secure I'm going to get you something to eat. What do you want?"

"I'm craving Chinese food. I love house special fried rice."

"Sounds good. I'll be back in a few."

***

She was sitting on the porch swing, swaying back and forth, enjoying being outdoors in the Georgia sun, when Jack returned with dinner.

"Here you go." He offered her a container with chopsticks and set the bag on the table next to the swing. "I'll get the drinks."

"Thank you."

This is the man I'll grow old with.

This is the man I want *to grow old with, the one who I need and who needs me.*

"Lemon water for the lady." He handed her the Styrofoam cup filled with ice and lemons.

"Thank you, again."

He sat down next to her and opened his container of moo goo gai pan. "Nice evening."

"It is."

Her cell phone rang.

She didn't answer.

"Aren't you going to take that call? I bet it's the office." He leaned back on the swing and extended his legs for it to sway.

"It can wait." She picked up her phone from the table next to her, turned it off and laid it back down.

Startled by her actions, Jack stopped the swing. "But you rarely turn off the phone."

She smiled at him. "I have more important things to do right now."

His mouth hung open for a minute, then he grinned. "Good," he shoveled a bite of his dinner in his mouth with his chopsticks.

"When did you learn how to use chopsticks? I have trouble with them sometimes."

"I have a Chinese friend from grade school who taught me how to use them. He also taught me a little Cantonese. Don't ask me what I remember." He laughed. "We're still friends today."

"Impressive." She smiled. He's a little worldlier than she thought.

He extended his knees and started the swing again slowly. She relaxed on his shoulder, held his hand and looked up at him.

"I thought I was going to miss this place. It's just a house. Not my home anymore."

He gazed down at her.

She felt the warmth of the slow Georgia breeze pass through her hair. He lifted his arm on the back of the swing and she moved closer to him.

"My home is with my family and the man who loves me."

He squeezed her shoulder and kissed her cheekbone just in front of her ear.

"And the man I love."

She reached her hand to his face and softly pressed her lips against his.

"Yes, I'll marry you."

CHAPTER 28

I'm getting married.

Again?

Those words echoed repeatedly in her head during the drive through rush hour traffic. She was on her way to Jack's house.

Soon to be *her* new home.

Her current house had an interested buyer. It would be sold soon.

God, the difference that semantics made.

She pulled in the driveway and waited a moment before going in.

Her new home.

It wasn't the baby that made her stomach turn over in excitement at the thought. "Home" just meant so much more than a house.

Home meant Jack and April and May and the little one in her belly.

Katie had a home…finally.

A new beginning. A ready-made family.

Something that she'd never experienced or expected, but what she'd always wanted.

A real family with conversations, places to go, movie nights, each other.

She'd been alone so long she couldn't imagine what living for others was going to be like, but she wanted it…badly.

She got out of the car, pressed a hand over her stomach and the light swell of the infant growing within her. With a smile, she walked to the door and wasn't surprised when it flew open before she could knock and April wrapped her arms around Katie's waist.

"I'm so glad you're here." She said excitedly.

May ran out of the kitchen and embraced Katie too. "Are you coming to live with us?" May asked.

"Are you getting married to my dad?" April asked.

"Ladies please let me have a seat." April and May released her and she took a few steps toward the couch. "On second thought I have to use the bathroom. I'll talk to both of you when I get out."

Both girls waited near the bathroom door when she opened it.

Each one of them beamed with excitement. May hopped up and down with her dark ponytails flinging through the air.

"Where's your dad?"

"He should be here any minute." April's voice answered anxiously. "Are you going to marry my dad? Please say yes please say yes, say yes, sayyessayyessayyes!"

Katie moved to the living room so she could sit down on her appointed spot on the couch and wait for Jack, like they'd said they would, so they could tell the girls together.

"We have to wait for your dad to get here. We'll talk about this at dinner. May, is everything all set? Do you need help with anything?"

April grinned. "No, ma'am, I'll help her. You stay here and rest. I'm calling Dad to tell him you're here then I'll help her finish with dinner."

April and May bounced off to the kitchen where Katie could hear the banging of the pots and pans.

The aroma of chili and homemade bread filled in the air and hunger pangs soon followed. Before she could ask for a piece of fruit, April brought her sweet tea and a buttered slice of homemade bread.

"I know dinner is in a little while but I thought you might be hungry."

Grateful for the kindness, Katie took small bites and sipped her tea. She was nervous but the sound of Jack's pickup truck pulling in the driveway interrupted her thoughts.

The keys rattled and the door opened.

He came to her first once he walked inside the house.

How was it possible that his smile made her heart flutter like that in her breast?

Jack extended his hand and Katie took it, allowed him to pull her to her feet, into his arms.

He tipped his head down and she closed her eyes, sank into his embrace, into the kiss.

"I'll be back down after I wash up and then we can tell the girls."

She smiled up at him. "Okay."

She made her way into the kitchen and the girls chatted about their day in camp. Twenty minutes later, he came into the kitchen and took a seat at the table next to Katie. He motioned for the girls to join them.

May hopped in her chair first and April turned off the stove and then sat down. Both of their faces were lit up with anticipated excitement. Jack broke the news.

"I've asked Katie to marry me."

Two sets of hopeful eyes turned to her face.

"And I've said yes."

Both girls howled at the news, jumped out of their seats, and ran around the table with hugs for everyone.

Katie's face glowed with happiness, although she still wondered what she'd gotten herself into. Jack managed a grin as well.

"When?" April asked.

"We're working out the details." Katie said.

May asked, "Am I going to have a sister? If so, can we name her June? Then we would have April, May, and June."

"I love that idea."

Katie looked across her place to catch Jack's eye, his arms around April while she hugged May, the small head tucked beneath her chin as the little girl sat on her lap, as naturally as anything in the world.

Jack smiled at her.

The crazy woman at the wedding had been wrong.

Katie wasn't getting the man who needed her.

She was getting the family she'd always wanted.

EPILOGUE

Jack and Katie stood at the altar at Dupree Country Club on a hot July afternoon gazing into each other's eyes. The minister motioned to Jack to say his vows. He pulled a sheet of paper out of his pocket.

"I wrote it down so I wouldn't forget anything."

A few people laughed including Katie. She warmly smiled at her husband-to-be.

He took a breath, crinkled the paper in his hand, and looked at the woman he loved. "Katie, as you know, my daughters and I were grieving when you came into our lives. The days were difficult for the three of us to move forward. When April came to me and asked me to come to a wedding and May told me that I would meet someone special, I thought the girls just wanted me to get out of the house."

There were polite chortles from the crowd, but he didn't care, didn't hear, his focus on the woman glowing before him.

"Since we met, you have unselfishly given your time to all of us and became such an integral part of our family that imagining life without you wasn't possible. Every day that you came by made life a little happier to live, made it a sunnier, more worthwhile. I didn't know I wanted or needed someone to love. I didn't know I was looking for that. I can't tell you how grateful I am that it found me. I didn't tell you the right way the first time I said I loved you. I promise to do better every day for the rest of our lives.

"I promise to love, honor and cherish you; to be your provider and your protector; to be your best friend and be faithful to you forever."

Katie fought back her tears, made to brush away the start of a fresh track though Jack beat her to it, his thumb a soft caress against her cheek, as loving as his words, the kind heart of the man she loved.

She cleared her throat, managed a smile that turned brighter every moment they stared at each other. "Jack, when I met you, I never imagined that we'd be standing here today taking our vows. You, April, and May welcomed me as part of your family and I was a complete stranger. You gave me a home I didn't know I was missing, you filled gaps in my heart I'd thought I'd hardened to ice. I needed you as much as you needed me. You showed me what my life was missing, what matters the most."

She shook her head, looked down at the pink and purple tulips back to his eyes. "You and I have come a long way since we met in growing and developing our relationship to what it is now. Careful planning by our little matchmakers," she glanced at her girls and they giggled with a smile, "has kindled our romance and the impending new birth sealed our destiny to be together forever. I will always love you, cherish you, and respect you as the only man in my life as long as we both shall live. I'm getting the man who needs me, and I'm getting the man I need in return."

***

Jack stepped onto the dance floor and waited for Don to twirl his daughter close enough that he could tap the older man, his father-in-law, on the shoulder and step in.

The gentleman smiled at Jack, a nod that conveyed respect and admiration, contentment.

Katie smiled in return, accepted the handing off from father to husband, placed her hand in Jack's and let him pull her into his arms.

"Would you like to dance?"

Katie grinned. "Just this one."

"All of them."

She stretched on her toes to touch her lips to his. "Always."

ABOUT THE AUTHOR

MIA MAE LYNNE - has enjoyed writing from the time she was in grade school. She started a diary and wrote in the journal for seven years. She always knew that one day all her creative ideas would come into fruition and writing has been her escape.

"The Chronicles of Fate" series was born in the metro Atlanta area allowing her to explore her creative side. The series was later renamed to "Southern Men Don't Fall in Love" with "Atlanta's Most Eligible Bachelor" as the first book in the series with many more to follow. She has enjoyed writing the series and has embraced each of the characters as they have entrusted her with their stories to share with the world.

After discovering psychic and mediumship abilities, she became a student of spiritualism. She has newly begun this path and has explored the traditional areas of tarot, numerology, astrology and other related areas of interest in the metaphysical arts. She has received training from the Fellowship of the Spirit in New York as well as read numerous books and attended various classes to expand her knowledge.